First Book of Frags

Dave Lordan

wurm press
wurmimapfel.net/press

ISBN: 978-0956373243
Wurm Press
77 Kilnacourt, Portarlington, Co. Laois, Ireland

wurmimapfel.net/wurmpress

*

Cover art by Adrian Reid:
http://cargocollective.com/orangeade

*

Read more at www.davelordanwriter.com or listen at http://davelordanpoet.bandcamp.com

Contents

Christmas Cracker

This weather we all have our own way of being born. Wiccan ceremonies. Underwater cameras. Strap-on midwives. Laughing gas in near space orbit. You name it, somebody has got to be online streaming it.

Well, I am a child of disaster like the rest of you, and this is my being-born story. It happened in a back-garden bedsit on the deep southside of Dublin around six weeks ago. It was the evening of the 25th of December at approximately twelve minutes past nine. 21:12. Two-one, one-two. That's a good one for the numerologists, isn't it? The mirrorologists even, but don't mind those fucking liars.

Before that there was Lizzie, the pediatric night-nurse, and Tom with the Van, her fella.

Lizzie was anaemic and underweight and bruised too easily. She always had welts and blotches ripening on her arms and legs. She occasionally sported a lumpy green or purple bruise so large and glossy you could mistake it for a leech. She had dizzy spells and headaches and she puked more often than she shat. The semi-circles under her eyes were grey somedays like military helmets. On other days they were stormcloud black. They could have carried lightning in them if they weren't so sad. She got these permanent black eyes from the nightshift at the hospital and from never ever sleeping at the weekend. And from worrying. Lizzie had always been a worrier. She had nearly always had something to worry about. These days most of her worrying was focused on Tom with the Van.

Like many Irish manuals, Tom with the Van was both muscular and gross. He had the shanks and shoulder-blades of a lean and well-worked horse, but a beach-ball midriff. His shape was therefore more seal-like, more amphibian, than fully bipedal. Nothing would have been more natural to Tom than to slop along mud-flats on his belly, half-in and half-out of the sea, propelled by his podgy, flipper-like arms. Especially if that sea was made of cider.

But by now he had been nearly three months off the piss. He was due to get his ninety day achievement key-ring at the lunchtime meeting of AA in St John of God's in Stillorgan on Stephen's Day. The fact that it was to be his fourth, or fifth, ninety day achievement medal, did not in any way detract from its significance. Or so he kept being told at the mass-length meetings by others slightly less brain-damaged than himself. 'Each day sober is a miracle for a drunk,' was one of the mantras the chorus of ex-and/or soon-to-be-again drunkards continuously drilled each other with, meeting after meeting, day after day, decade upon decade. A miracle! Miraculous Tom! The miracle of Tom, of Tom with the Van. It had a ring to it, didn't it?

While stuck in traffic mornings, afternoons, and evenings during the weeks leading up to the holidays, Tom found himself daydreaming a lot about receiving the keyring and the uplifting ritual applause that would accompany it. This was the motivation he needed to make it through the excruciatingly boozy holiday season without leaping off the wagon. He luxuriated in the dozens of encouraging hugs and congratulatory handshakes he had coming to him from tweedy old-timers, the ones who stood in silent rooms in boxy homes before secretly laughing mirrors, shining up their liver-stains like the character-giving blotches on wooden antiques, before marching out to preach the sober way to the demented. These old missioners promised him that everything they had could be his, if only he stayed away from that first drink, a day at a time, or a minute at a time if needs be, for the rest of his life. It was that simple, that rewarding.

Everyone with an input—counsellors, family, boss, mates—said Tom was doing well. He even said so himself, quite regularly.

'I'm doing well, amn't I not?' he would inquire of Lizzie, softly, as they were drifting off to sleep together after a long joint and a short ride, each leaving one lazy eye open to be mesmerised by the glutinous gyrations of the lava-lamp, or to stare up at the slime-green luminous stars a previous tenant had stuck to the ceiling.

'Yes, you're doing well,' she told him. 'Very well indeed, babes. Keep it up now though won't you not?'

'I will. Don't you worry, love of mine.'

Then they would squeeze each other's sticky hands and gaze into each other's bloodshot eyes and maybe even go at it again, or at least think about going at it again.

Because of Tom's new sober reliability, Christmas Day was going to be very special this year. The nearest thing to a declaration of intentions. An engagement to be engaged, sort of. If everything worked out, only good things would follow for the two of them. Not that they would be getting married or anything as old-fashioned or uneconomical as that. They would just move on to the stage many of their friends were already at, saving up for a deposit for a house together. And, yes, Lizzie had an idea of where, at a stretch, they might be able to afford, and some ideas on interior decoration, and on what organic greens would sprout out of the tidy drillrows in the vegetable and herb garden out the back.

The agreed Christmas Day timetable was as follows: Tom with the Van would collect his mom from the home in the morning as soon as the 8 o'clock Yuletide mass in there had ended. Then he would van her to Glasnevin graveyard to say hello to all her friends and relations. Then they would zip down to Lizzie to start into the ceremonial meal at midday on the dot.

Tom kept telling Lizzie how much he was looking forward to sharing the first Christmas of his new life with the female of his dreams:

'A recovering drunk is supposed to have one happy vision to focus on and keep him sober. whenever thoughts of booze assault him I always think of sitting by an open fire with one arm around the woman who brought me into the world, and the other around the woman I hope and pray will be seeing me out of it. I imagine us there in the heat and glow, cuddling and chatting and keeping each other company, forever and ever.'

'Aw shucks, I'm so touched to be one half of your antibooze charm,' said Lizzie, and she meant it.

Tom broke out on Christmas Eve. The mother never got collected from the home on Christmas morning. She didn't notice. She was past noticing anything. Lizzie tried ringing Tom dozens of times, always going straight to message. Then she started ringing round friends for clues and traces. No one knew anything, or so they said. She heard a lot of children in the background of the calls, laughing, crying, babbling, whining.

The last time she tried Tom's mobile she found the messaging service's language had changed, the accent having deepened in an easterly direction, towards somewhere a lot colder and darker than here. She hung up, quitting the Tomhunt, switched off the phone and exiled it to the very bottom of her handbag, burying it under tampons and condoms and fags and codeines and a jumble of other spares and necessaries.

She sat on the beanbag in front of the TV eating brandy-soaked pudding out of a plastic bowl. Then she drank the wine and vodka she had been hiding from Tom. No need to hide it anymore. Around nine o'clock in the evening she had a paralytic tantrum and tore the burnt turkey to shreds, spreading it in bits and pieces all over the kitchen-cum-dining-cum-living-cum-bedroom. Stuffing got plastered to the violet lightshade, the window-sill, the Seraphim atop the plastic tree.

Then Lizzie started keening like a stone church full of island widows after all the curraghy men have been smashed to unrecoverable pieces by a freak wave, by a malicious heave from the deep striking up through a deceivingly tranquil sea.

Outside the bedsit, through concrete and hedgerow and drizzle, cats, rats, pigeons, crows and foxes fled in all directions from Lizzie's ear-splitting grief.

A few minutes later, at the very apex of her screeching, at precisely 21:12, Lizzie picked up a glossy blue Marks and Spencer Christmas cracker, embroidered with gold-foil constellations, and featuring an artist's impression of the three wise men, the tall one wearing sunglasses, and pulled it between her left and right hands. Against the odds her left hand won. But that fact failed to register because of what she saw ballooning into existence out of the Christmas cracker, which was me. In my birthday suit, of course, except for the cocaine: I was covered from head to foot in cocaine. A snowman indeed, and an impressive sight I assure you. I had some cocaine-coated cock on me, for a young lad.

Now Lizzie was in total shock, without a doubt, and croaking and spluttering something like a thousand Amazonian toads being put through a wine press. Pan-de-fucking-moany-um, what?

When she recovered herself a bit she started to lick, to lick off my cocaine caul. She licked my soles and my ankles and in between my toes. She licked my heels, my calves, my knees and thighs, my ass-crack and balls, my belly-button and my nipples and underneath my arms. She licked my eyelids and my nostrils and the inside of my ears. She licked every last particle of cocaine off my hair. She licked and licked until all the cocaine had been licked off me and until her tongue was as dry and white and hard as a stick of chalk.

Then she had a seizure.

I know most people are going to say the least I could have done is stuck around and kept poor Lizzie company while she was dying, since it was the depth of her rage and misery and her utter futility that gave birth to me. But look at the state of most people. Most people are in no position to give the likes of me advice. And if there's one thing I can't stand it's moral whining, especially from grown-ups. The best anyone can expect out of this dump planet is to get our hardcore thrills from it, right?

What's the point in saying or doing otherwise? Tenderness and all that shite is for hypocrites and mealy-mouthed muffin-heads.

I'm with Blake when he says 'Drive your cart and your plow over the bones of the dead.'

So, without a moment's dallying, I said my goodbyes to Mom. Then, right after I took my first ever indoor piss-in-a-corner, I quickly donned Tom with the Van's red-and-white Christmas costume. It made me look like a crash-diet Santa Claus on account of its superior girth. I also took Lizzie's iPod and the Bose headphones she had bought herself for Christmas - her only present, as it turned out. They were part of my inheritance after all. Then I put on the techno loud, real loud, like the battledrums of Beelzebub, and then I fucked off in search of a rave or a brothel and someone to screw.

I've been having a fucking ball of a time ever since, telling all the twisted skags I meet at parties and bridewells and prison cells just how it is I got born.

Dr Essler's Cocaine

Let me confide in you. Last Thursday, Betty, my sister-in-law, drowned in the hotel swimming pool. She was out of her mind on Dr Essler's cocaine, which we at the central committee had been partaking of all afternoon. Poor Betty; she served the drinks and the tidbits and every time she swung by we gave her a little sniff. Central committee meetings are always very spirited affairs and high-jinx often occur, especially towards nightfall as the serious business is dispatched and we begin to bat around minor agenda items in which no one is too invested. Betty has always been our entertainment as well as our host at these events, which we obviously have to close off from the Irish staff and the local musicians we would normally hire. Eventually, with her husband's approval, we asked Betty, a great beauty, to titillate us by removing one item of clothing every time she returned with a round. As you can appreciate, the periods between when I got up to strike the bong for refreshments became shorter and shorter and Betty closer and closer to full nudity.

Dr Essler also increased the size and the frequency of his doses. Dr Essler, by the way, is what the English call a card. He has his cocaine delivered to Killybegs in the County Donegal by monthly submarine in the very same briefcase as our Berlin instructions.

Before long, the amount of pent-up energy in the room could have provided electricity for a small nation. Something had to be done to relieve it. I did not want a repeat of the occasion at the youth camp on the hotel grounds in '34. We had all had a super evening of folksong and wrestling, buoyed up by an endless supply of Dr Essler's cocaine. Unfortunately, the hotel and grounds descended into a state of riot because of an insulting comment about Leni Riefenstahl thrown out by a fifteen-year-old oik of a Rottenführer from a marsh hamlet near Kiel.

It happened that after only half an hour of our game Betty had gone from a concealed 'French' maid to a fully revealed 'Grecian' one. Naked and positively gleaming, she carried in yet another tray of whiskey thimbles and served each man in turn at his place. I ordered her to be at her ease and to remain with us a while in the committee room. We had had enough to drink and eat for now. Without removing our uniforms or regalia, we took turns fucking her in a most frenzied but comradely cocaine-inspired manner. What pleasure we had of her was indescribable. She too was in her element. She groaned and whimpered and pleaded for us to empty ourselves into and over her.

After this had been done to everyone's complete satisfaction I ordered Betty to unblind the bay window. In the grounds and woods the Celtic night was moonlit and mystical and silvery. The hillsides sparkled through their seams of quartz, and the bare granite hilltops were burnished and regal under the moon like the places of ancient worship they most certainly were, places ever-belonging to high-kings and druids and ever-inspiring to the poets of this misty, fact-despising land where I've been posted. I fell into a reverie over the trees. The fir trees seemed like enormous vertebrae, like the planted skeletons of whales. Then I thought of the undersides of an ancient fleet, the thousands of galley slaves, rowing, rowing towards the destiny of nations, towards the edge of the world. The yew trees reminded me of tribal statues facing out to sea, outlasting by centuries the people that had built them and yet to remain unvisited for centuries to come. Who knows what these lost people really meant by their statues, heh? When a people dies out in disaster they and their symbols become nothing more than matter for speculation, for poetry. Meaning, too, is a victor's prerogative.

The copper beeches were aggressively colourful. They were native pig-chiefs with endless hair and trinkets and too proud by far. I made a mental note to have them uprooted and chopped into firewood. The monkey puzzles were a flagrant picture of inutile disorder. They put me in mind of mangled or failed machinery, of things purposeless, shapeless, directionless and failed. The family who planted and tended the arboretum were aristocratic decadents. Their taste for the sick and the 'curious' form is everywhere obvious. Sometimes I think the arboretum, in all its senselessness and disarray, could only have been designed by Edward Lear, the nonsense rhymester, whose work is the clearest expression of what happens to the souls of those with long and cosseted lives and with no heroic quest to pursue.

The arboretum is proof that the English are a race on which culture has been totally wasted. It is a standing embarrassment to me, but it will not be allowed to last. Dr Essler, himself a woodland enthusiast and a published author on the matter of forest management, is in the process of educating me in the noble tree species and how to source and encourage them. I will fill my estate with the upright trees of the world, the ones that built strong ships and chariots and fueled the ancient furnaces of war.

Amid all that nature, the swimming pool shone numinously, a defiantly regular shape cut into the earth by human ingenuity. Through genius and graft—genius standing over graft, with an abacus in one hand and a stout whip in the other—we have reached a higher plane than nature alone could ever do.

I suggested that Betty, to clean herself off, should go and take a swim, and that we would watch her a while cooling off in our own way.

We all stood wordlessly by the window watching her alluringly enter the pool, like a glimmering nymph sent down as a gift by Diana. She was the colour of and bewitching like the moon and Dr Essler's cocaine. She was the moon and Dr Essler's cocaine in human form. Back and forth the length of the pool she went, back and forth, her thrusting arms and legs flashing in the silver light, mesmerising all of us. And then, suddenly, she started to flail. Of course we all thought it was part of the show; Betty was nothing if not inventive in that regard. You know what it looked like to me? It looked like something enormous had hooked her through the midriff and was trying to pull her out of the water, some giant fisher from a hell-fleet in the lunar-tinted clouds, some demon perched on the crown of a cedar with a rod designed for human flesh and souls.

And then as suddenly, she stopped. She stopped and went under the surface of the pool. As she went down the ripples from her flailing were still pulsing madly and irregularly to the poolsides, then rebounding. Each wave-front met and crashed through the rebound of its predecessor, carrying on weakened but nevertheless all the way to the edge, where it in turn switched its allegiances to attack the oncoming wave. This is what we all were now fascinated by, meditating on such subjects as force and reaction, wave-power as a means of energetic transaction, the great successes and great failures of charge tactics in the nineteenth century, the control of large swathes of territory by transmission from a central point of strength, the endless surging forth of new phenomenon through time, the continuous undulating poem of reality, the submarines bristling with terror beneath pacific surfaces, history as martial narrative with carnival interludes, forgetting about Betty for a little while.

Until she resurfaced. Maybe twenty minutes had passed in reverie. She was at the centre of the pool, arms and legs spread, as if served to our gazing by giants of the hills. Her stomach had noticeably swollen. I speculated that in her underwater absence, which seemed so brief to us, she had spent months in a Neptunian world and become pregnant by a tyrant of the mermen. As one of the volk in which the race of men intersects with the race of Gods, this fancy of exalted miscegenation greatly pleased me. I shared it with my comrades and they spontaneously applauded.

Shortly after, having once again indulged ourselves in a steeply uplifting dose of Dr Essler's remarkable cocaine, we took off outdoors to join Betty. Wouldn't it be fun to have another howling orgy out there in the pool? Of course it would. Betty would surely agree, given how she was lying there like an advertisement for pool orgies.

First to reach her in the water was Oberführer McMahon. He yelped with the cold shock of rubbing nakedly against her. Her condition was confirmed by another two comrades, who had already been on the way to her before the yelp, and they dragged her to the poolside and laid her out. For a long time we stood huddled around her not knowing what to do or to think. Of course the wickedest thoughts went through everyone's heads but we stood our ground against our baser impulses, despite how clear it was to all of us that something extra-licentious was going to have to take place to get us back on our high for the rest of the night. Everyone's dignity was fully retained.

As if coming out of trance, after maybe half an hour of gazing at the naked body of a pale and glinting lunar-queen, Bishop O' Donovan knelt to the body and began performing the last rites. Dr Essler meanwhile went back into the house to retrieve some more cocaine and a death certificate from his briefcase. As soon as we had all had some cocaine to bring us back to our senses I suggested that we carry Betty back into the hotel and have her lie in state there in her own room while we figured out the arrangements. As soon as this was carried out I rang ********** in Dublin and arranged for the discreet delivery of the most ornate coffin immediately available. I also made sure with ********** that there would be no other complications. The death would be legally recorded as accident, we would bury her privately on the grounds, and there would be no public mention of it. I do not wish to exaggerate about the Celts or wax on their sensibilities but I do feel a certain pride and indeed gratitude in having been posted to a country where the techniques of silencing are even further along in some respects than our own. Not only could such a thing as happened with Betty not have taken place in the Irish countryside, it could not even be imagined to have taken place. Mention of it would not be interpreted as political subversion but as mental illness through and through. No official sense would be made of it. No official response except against the person or persons making such obscene and ludicrous claims. In Ireland telling the truth is a symptom of madness. *Say nothin' to no one about nothin' at all and sure won't you get along grand* is how Paddy the old gardener puts it and it's almost a national slogan. The wit of the Irish is that of the cunning weakling who knows just how weak he really is by comparison. Their commoners work like mules for little reward besides avoiding starvation, and deal with any resentment this causes by drowning it and by beating their wives, their children and dogs.

Really, for our kind of people Ireland is the safest country imaginable. The Irishman does not care what his masters get up to as long as he is allowed to get drunk and lash out at his own. I am going off the point but doesn't it make you so happy that this race of self-hating inebriates defeated the English? Our war with London will not last long.

*

But all this is by the by except to explain how the position of Hotel Manageress has once again become available. I hope your client remains interested. The members of the central committee have examined her credentials, and her photographs, which we thank you most heartily for supplying. We do think that she has all the required characteristics, although we would like to be finally reassured about the matter of obedience. You write that as a young girl she may be frightened of travel and leaving home. Have an extra 200 Marks for the difficulties of persuading her. Besides that, offer 100 Marks to her father and her nervousness will soon fall away. Tell the girl that being here would at least get her away from the war, which won't be long coming now. Whenever it does get going I and most of the other comrades will be heading in the opposite direction, to join in the fight for the Fatherland. We have already made preparations with ****** for that. So things will not normally be as exciting as during Betty's tenure. We don't want you to lead your client astray on this matter. Hotel managing is boring drudgery with carnival interludes. However, Doctor Essler, as our most senior diplomat, will be remaining in Hibernia for the duration and will be often at the hotel, where a smaller group will meet under his direction to keep the Irish Party going, with the idea of massive expansion as soon as our total victory becomes clear. Dr Essler will be an important man in the Irish province of the Reich. As the Hotel Manageress's immediate senior he will be sure to look after her in every possible way.

Kathleen is just a word we'll never settle

When Kathleen came home my father died.

When Kathleen took off her clothes at the wake I saw, for the very first time, the whole of the island of Ireland.

Conversations about Kathleen.

Kathleen staring in an oily puddle in a bog, comparing herself to money; notes and coins: weight, texture, shape, mobility and so on. As well as that, she forgets things, and the names of things. Whatever is not tied on to her she forgets. For months now, I have been calling my mortgage Kathleen.

As for the harp, most of the time Kathleen has no one to carry it. It must stay in the house of the nobles she plays for when broke and dejected.

At a party in Doolin, where Kathleen floats around, a change to the ukulele is suggested.

Kathleen tells lies all night at the party but everyone believes her. *It's your face* said the Donegal actor under the yew, walking her home through the graveyard at dawn. Everyone enchanted just nods.

Kathleen remembers the nod of the enchanted the next time she sees it.

Kathleen reels in a flash-bellied trout on a Monaghan lake the colour of greased tin. The aluminium rain passes through her. Neutrinos in billions pass through her.

Kathleen has a crush on the North.

Kathleen's perched on the wall of an Urlingford garage eating half of a sausage, the other half she gave to an Urlingford crow that sat down beside her.

Kathleen scavenges. She finds Zola in the bin. She boils dandelions. She knows where to harvest periwinkles in the winter months; she knows how to prepare them and eat them without poisoning herself. She has kept more than herself alive with this knowledge.

She tries hitching to Derry but by Longford she's wrecked and so she breaks into a derelict hotel to sleep it off in a four poster crawling with ants she doesn't heed. The next morning her head is at her so she traipses towards Mass for the noise and the company. A man in black tweed in the doorway gives her a cigarette. *It's a funeral of a suicide* he says. *D'ya fancy a pint?* Kathleen is not too sure of herself here.

Kathleen put ten thousand into the post office in Dundalk but came back in a ski-mask and with her cousin's first sawn-off an hour later to rob it all back.

Kathleen paints landscapes with pylons and hawks, but others don't see them like that.

Kathleen keeps a rained-on mattress in the woods surrounded by empty wine bottles. The next time she attends at the nobles' house she gifts them a black and white photograph of this, which they frame and hang in the music room, in view of the harp.

Kathleen knows that her life is a kind of antique that will be paused over and traded for centuries hence.

Kathleen plays harp as if her fingers are dreaming a new, beautiful world into being. In a lapse between melodies, while the dreaming lingers, she tells a story about an Irish monk a thousand years ago who trusted completely in God. The monk set himself adrift into the Atlantic on a small rowing boat without a map or provisions or any idea of a destination. He wished only to end up wherever God mysteriously chose to direct him and to build there a church of bare stone in which to worship in fervid solitude for the rest of his days. Nobody knows, or at least nobody says, if the monk ended up in America or Iceland or Madagascar, or at the bottom of the sea. Nobody knows if he kept his covenant to God or if he gave in to the devil on the battering waves, promising his soul in return as long as the devil saved him from drowning. Nobody knows if he was back where he set out the next morning and quit his vows in dismay, or if he came back fifty years later without aging a day, speaking Old Flemish and Maths, a fearsome, inscrutable changeling.

Any one of thousands of outlying ruins could be his. *Was not the sea at the time full of such monks on the drift, common as mackerel in those crazy-visioned days?* said a member of the audience. *About that I don't know a thing* said Kathleen. *But I do know that I too am a drifter by faith, trusting in the unknown holiness that lies ahead of us, just beyond our reach.*

Kathleen feels pity for the peasantry of Europe in the fourteenth century. She sees them in her head at night, alone in their fields and their hovels, at war with all nature, all the animals and man.

When the soldiers come to the village scouting for conscripts, Kathleen dresses up her uncles as her aunties and they nearly get away with it. Her aunties have already been taken away and discarded by soldiers from one of the other sides in the war. Kathleen tells the soldiers on the way to the base that *we can only survive by pretending*. She says *we must try to do what the dead would do in our places, if they could ever come back. We must behave as if the dead are watching and waiting to receive us or else we are lost. It all comes down in the end to the dead* says Kathleen. *Are they coming or going? Are they present or absent?*

Kathleen on the boat with hundreds of others, cast off with no destination.

Kathleen pressed in a throng behind a wire fence with her stumps stretched through it. The people on behalf of the angels are giving her presents of chocolate and soap. Her eyes are still beautiful. Her white little teeth are beautiful and sad.

A Bill

Friends, neighbours, townspeople and all passing and concerned. Quick explanation and friendly request: With the decline of transport it is as if places have grown further apart. In other words, the country has grown bigger, and there are fewer and fewer visitors, there is less and less moving about. There is little or no circulation at all. In isolated districts in the mountains and deep countryside there are settlements that no one has either visited or departed from for years. One wonders how the people survive in these inland islands, so far from the influence and the stewardship of more important places. What they eat; how they distract themselves; what exotic new diseases and mutations and neuroses and marital customs are arising among them. We talk about such things a lot in my circle, being naturally so much more interested in other people's lives than we are our own.

Virtually the only thing that moves between settlements now which isn't bearing decrees and heavy sentences is the wind. The wind which carries only seeds, viruses and rumours. The rumour grows now (and what do rumours grow into but facts we must act on?) of the first town, within our national borders, to be completely depopulated by suicide. Although to say 'completely depopulated by suicide' could never be strictly medically correct. Everyone with a serious and genuine interest in the subject realises and admits this. There must have been accidents too as well as 'natural', or at a stretch 'misadventurous,' deaths. Suicide in many cases can be as difficult as euthanasia to prove. The difference between a trip and a leap, a misdose and an overdose, an accidental crash and a deliberate collision with a wall, is often impossible to tell. There is also 'slow suicide', an intriguing category which is normally thought to fundamentally apply only to addicts but is broadening all of the time as research into the phenomenon increases. Slow suicide covers anyone who consciously or unconsciously commits an act, or commits an omission of an act, or allows any act or omission of an act to be committed against them, which might increase their chances of dying out before their natural span, in which case we are all suicides, differing from each other only in our choice of timescale, whether sudden or protracted. There is also the obvious question of whether the species as a whole is committing suicide, whatever percentage of its constituent members can be decided as doing so. *Homo Sapiens Suicide*. And then there is the cosmic or metaphysical realm to worry about. Is the human species an attempt by the planet, or even the universe as a whole, to completely do away with itself? Any such line of enquiry leads of course to cosmic intentions and cosmic intentions are God. Is humanity the suicide method of God? So, as you see, there is endless matter for discussion, debate and multi-disciplinary research. I am certain that this new suicide town will become an international centre for such.

The last person to die over there in Suicide Town was almost certainly a suicide. The majority of its final hundred or two-hundred-wave of deaths was done-by-self, no doubt. This is enough to qualify the town for its unique and everlasting position. The nearest rivals are thirty or forty suicides behind, and mass suicides in order to break records *do not count* in any case. There can be no two first places in matters of historical record. The town in question is the equivalent of the site of a famous miracle, or a religious apparition. Think of the city of Padua, or the village of Knock, and how, over the centuries, those two very holy, unique places, have benefited from their very holy uniqueness. Suicide Town will also be, no doubt, a place of dark pilgrimage providing much needed and long-lasting employment for thousands at least.

Here in our own morbid town of survivors, we have nothing so grand to distinguish us. Our town is full of doped-down morons with nothing to live for, unable to raise the enthusiasm to kill themselves. Most of our citizens, in the words of one local wit, have the potential of the average stone. Someone must pick us up, some force must budge us for any motion to occur. We go absolutely nowhere on our own. Can you blame the active sections of the youth for wanting out?

The high-achieving town of the suicides, which I shall not name (for fear of many things, including spectres and legal compromise) has within a very short time of space assumed a mystical reputation and an irresistible draw, like an Atlantis of shadows, among a certain few seekers, me among them. We want to set out for, and see with our own eyes, this overground catacomb where life is shuffled off with expertise and death has an appetite like a thousand pot-bellied pigs. The Paris of the mortuaries! The Venice of the mental plague! At long long last there is something out of the ordinary to reach for in the hope of being transformed. Which has finally given me—the adventurer of the second hand settee—the excuse and the push that I needed. In just one veritable Blitzkrieg of a week I have given up Ponstan, porno, caffeine and weed. I'll take no congratulations for what I should obviously not have gotten into in the first place, but you understand the state we are all in and the effort I have gone through all the same. Besides this, I have begged, borrowed, stolen and finally bought the last mule in our parish—the bookie's own beloved mule of fortune.

Tomorrow I intend striking out *da solo* for Suicide Town. However, there is room for one more on my saddle if there really is someone who thinks they can take the arduous, discomforting ride. Understand, however, that you would join me not as a partner in the venture, at least not at first, but in a subordinate role. I will be Heritage Director of Suicide Town. I will be Suicide Director of Heritage Town. I will manage, recruit, inspire and above all organise the award-winning exhibitions and the expert, enthusiastic staff. I will programme summer concerts of suicide music. I want to be the one who explains the great phenomenon to visiting personages, and to the hordes, when large-scale international transport returns, as it must. The innovative conceptual expertise which I have amply demonstrated above, backed up by my total command of the empirical data, qualifies me above all others for the post. I foresee no serious challenges or challengers, as long as I can make it out of here and across to Suicide Town. I am entitled to this dream and to my attempt to realise it. I do not expect any of you to wish me success but I must entreat you at least to not, out of envy or spite, attempt to prevent me from leaving.

The Fucking Titanic

A selection of testimony from non-survivors.

I held my son's head under the water until he drowned so that he wouldn't die alone out there. Also, the screaming is not something you would want a young child to hear. Some people meet death with mild composure, but others make a big production of it. It's like a singsong in a beer-hall in Hell out here. The demons that live in the top of our voices. But I don't believe in Hell. I believe in swift decisions, and the terrible choices we must make for our children. I made mine. My child I did not fail.

*

Some toff shot me when I rushed the boat, and I bled to death on deck in seconds flat. I only wanted space made for my wife and child. The boat had space but not for ruffians. My wife and child watched me die. My wife in tears. My child silent, terrified. I haven't had any news of them since. Have you?

*

I am a philosopher. I try to think about what things mean. I try to assign meaning to things. Everything means something. Everything that is can be assigned a meaning. Meaning is how everything speaks to everything else. Meaning is how we force a confession out of things. Without meaning there is no comprehension, no communication, just silence inside, and chaos in-between. There is silence inside and chaos in-between, but this is called horror or vertigo and cannot be safely approached or admitted, causing madness and suicide, panic and shell-shock and incapacity if it so happens to be.

In the final moments of our life we might feel our consciousness dissolve as we are being readmitted into the blissfully meaningless flow of the world, as we sink away from thought and words and images and sense into the ungraspable, the formless, becoming liquid ourselves again, rejoining the flux indivisible.

Why meaning? Because division. Because we are split. Because we have gained ourselves and lost the cosmos. Because longing. Because helplessness. Because terror and need. Because complexity. Because life at the higher end needs so much protection and guaranteed energy supply. The baby is born screaming for voices and milk. We look for a nurturing giant who knows how things work, who can explain things, who knows what 'milk' is and how to dispense it. The nurturing giant already knows what the baby means by its screams, and chooses how to respond, with love or perversity. And the more we know the more we want. Longing and knowledge are conjoined. They mutually generate and increase. They are not opposites, as is sometimes claimed. Everything is known that is wanted to be known. When we cease to long, we cease to know as well.

I am sorry to lecture, but I find that it calms. I am tossed by waves with spikes and claws and nails of ice in them, and my ears are full of wailing. I have a longing for calm. Do you understand?

How cold the water is. How numb and tired my limbs are. How I am running out of energy to breathe. How I wish now that I could not understand what is happening to me. Unconsciousness come now, come now and release me.

While I am waiting erotically for death, I think about all the things that would save me from death if they could. Like an ancient god, if I were one of the favoured. My dead father, if he were a powerful ghost. The lifeboat passing by over there, if I had had a first class ticket. Death speaks to us in simple present tense: either you are or you are not. But life, constantly forking, and at constant risk, prefers the subjunctive. What if? What if I had somehow failed to get on board? What if I had not been born to die? Or my father not been born? What if I were rich, not broke? What if I were a fish? What if I had wings? Everything is down to chance. Everyone is born pregnant with a ghost they can't get rid of, a ghost that they must carry to full term. See the lifeboat over there? I hear them praying in their murmurous gratitude. The boats full of people rowing are like centipedes upside down in the water, waving their legs. They think they are saved. But no one is saved. They are all going the same way as I, though they may reach dry land before they drown. Let them. Life is a flailing, however long it lasts, however luxurious.

Meaning tries to fly away from death, but cannot fly. From one doomed skull to another it flees, until the last mind drowns.

*

Where is my mammy gone?

*

No, no, no, I forgive no-one. Not the innocent nor guilty do I forgive. Not the high nor the low nor the middling sort I forgive. Everything that lives I hate and blame.

Pageantman! Lady of the brooch and prayerbook! I abhor your pious masquerade. How dare you celebrate my agony. How dare you forgive on my behalf the unforgivable. That you may choke on your prayers for my peaceful repose. How can you imagine that I am at rest? I died in freezing abandonment. Hypothermia and a heart-attack. My toddler screaming in my ear. Which was the greater pain, the ice that thousand-stabbed me in the marrow of my bones, or my child's wailing terror in my heart, my ears? I cannot tell. These are my final moments. I have no others to share. I have no peace, no rest forever. I wish the same agonies for you, and ten times worse. I wish you into the whirlpool, the hurricane, the tidal-wave, the torpedo-strike, the superbomb. I wish you cancer. I wish you militias. I wish you trampled by horses. I wish you struck by a train. I wish you arthritis of the spine. I wish you a fall onto railings or rocks far beneath. For you I am down in the root of the sea switching the currents round to kick off a superstorm. For you I take lightning into my sea-bitten eyes and cast it into gaps where continents meet, hoping to crack them apart. For you I blow great overturning waves at fishing boats. For you I creep along the inner shore looking for lone swimmers to tug down.

Pageantman! Lady of the brooch and prayerbook! I am your enemy. When I meet you in eternity I will rip you in half.

I can wait. A billion years is the same thing as one where I am. There are ten billion chambers in my flowing tomb and then there are none. In each of ten billion rooms my child screeches for me and in each one she is always alone. I can never find her. When I get there she is gone. Always alone. Let the pageants burn! Let the brass bands be swallowed by a trough. Let moth holes perforate the bunting. Let the wavers on the shoreline wave themselves backwards into a tomb. Let the shipyards disintegrate. Let termites gnaw the magnates in their sleep. Let barnacles with acid lips eat all the hulks. Let all the fleshly liquify and freeze.

A quality of spinning. A quality of being spun. Who is the captain? Who is the president now? London will sink and Queenstown be forgot. Goodbye England. Goodbye USA. Southampton goodnight. You're joining me soon. Spin within spin. Trough within trough. Sea within sea. Death within death. Drown within drown. Shall I write you a ballad? Death is the tune and the instrument time. And I am the song. I am the song of disaster. I am the iceberg song. Even the sea itself will drown in time. I in the sea will drown and the sea itself will drown in time.

*

Imagine it is true that when you die a sorrowful death you end up in Utopia.

A heaven of more or less your own design.

Imagine you find out the truth about everything, and everything makes perfect sense.

Imagine that all is forgiven. No fatigue. No cynics. No guilt. Utter shamelessness. Bliss.

Imagine joy and solidarity and all you love, no disease, no spreading death, nothing ever to fear.

Imagine that there nothing is lost; nothing is broken. And all the world's lost things are found.

And all the broken are remade there.

No human sorrows there. No human desolation.

Where there is no death no pain no longing to escape. No action. Imagine.

Imagine all that forgetting. All that denial. All that repression.

Imagine whom all this bullshit might really be serving.

Imagine.

Street Party

In the midst of the chaos my father and his friends decided to set up a roadblock at the entrance to the estate.

After a quarter of an hour the police came along but they were fired at and they retreated in no time.

They came back an hour later with many reinforcements but my father's ranks had also swelled and a deal was made. The police were not allowed to approach the estate and my father's militia would not fire upon them unless they did so. Nor would my father attempt to extend his power beyond the estate. My father had no intention of abiding by this last clause, but he knew he had to buy himself some time by appearing to sincerely agree to it. My father understood that for conquering one needs not only numbers but also the loyalty which gives ranked numbers cohesion and purpose. Loyalty could not be forced. It had to be nurtured, and time and care this would take.

Within hours the roadblock had become the hub of a carousel of spontaneous neighbourliness. Generators and spotless, well-stocked portaloos appeared as if they had been coaxed into being by the inspirational presence of the roadblock. Up to now most of the inhabitants of our humdrum, pebble-dashed exurb had been as alien and uncommunicative to each other as to lamp-eyed creatures of the ocean deep. My father's ingeniously decisive act transformed us. Despite the estate being nearly ten years old, it was the first time many of the residents had ever properly met each other. Many people were complimenting my father for finally being the one to take some initiative, bringing everyone on the estate together in the natural way. The general sentiment was 'why haven't we done this before?' and 'I hope this roadblock is the first of many.'

Several marquees were set up offering warm shelter, interesting home-cooked food, relaxing non-alcoholic drinks, comfortable seating and entertainment of various kinds. A children's space scheduled storytelling, face-paints and a kite-making workshop. Mrs Tealy, the Wiccan, set up her own palmreading tent, which my father grudgingly allowed. Permission for an ecumenical prayer service was sought and granted. A temporary tennis court and chess tournament were set up. An attempt was made to open a brothel but my father got wind and had it immediately shut. The instigator was brought before the supreme court of the roadblock, whereby my father heard the case and passed a sentence of death-by-everyone.

Everyone was surprised at the weapons everybody else was holding in reserve just in case something like this ever happened. There was a wide range of hand-guns and shotguns, machetes and daggers, bows and arrows. Several people had those irritating laser-pointers and indiscriminately waved them around, until my father ordered a halt. One man brought his paintball kit, still boxed since a Christmas some years ago. He was good-naturedly derided by all. As well as this my father ordered that a stockpile of broken bricks, slate, and stone be brought up to the roadblock from the builder's mess at the back of the estate—the one never cleared up despite thousands of promises.

My father was extremely pleased when the stockpile posse returned with a digger and steamrolling machine, but he immediately began to fret about diesel supplies. As he was pacing back and forth trying to figure this out, one of the men with the laser pointers placed a red dot in the middle of his ribcage. My father strolled over to the man, who was brazenly smirking, and beat him into the ground until he was unconscious and sounded as if he was choking. My father then hopped up into the steamrolling machine and began rolling back and forth over the man until he had been utterly flattened into the road. When my father first started doing this people cheered, then after a while they only looked on in awe, and when he finally stopped and dismounted from the steamrolling machine they gave him a standing ovation which lasted for nearly a quarter of an hour. There was nothing of the man left now but a faint image, like a watermark and my father ordered it covered over with lime.

By this time the television channels showed nothing but large crowds holding up posters and placards in support of whoever owned the particular channel. This could get confusing because television channels often changed hands during the chaos. But when you thought about it, it wasn't really all that confusing. I used to watch the demonstrations to see how many people I could spot holding up placards in support of now-ascendant politicians whom hours or days previously the crowds had been screeching mortal threats against; there were plenty. It dawned on me that the crowds were in fact TV channel employees; when you took over the channel, you got them into the bargain.

Actual news came intermittently over foreign frequencies on the radio, from places in whose interests it was to issue a factual (I do not say 'truthful') report of the meanderings in our chaotic land. Since morning the national government had twice fallen and twice been replaced. This was nothing special in those days.

At around 4 o clock in the evening a man on a bicycle with a white flag attached to the right handlebar approached the roadblock. Strangely, he appeared to us all to be gliding along about a fifth of a metre above the bicycle path. He was honking his horn at regular intervals, which sounded like a kind of code or message. Everyone recognised him as once having served in a national government as minister for bicycles. According to news reports he had been assassinated months before, but he could easily have paid the news to put out the assassination report for his own reasons. My country was full of zombie politicians who died and came back from the dead; revenance was both a profile and a vote booster. It was suggested that he was coming to negotiate with us and may even have been sent by the mischievous local chief of police to persuade us to dismantle the roadblock. When he had come within twenty metres of the front prow of the roadblock and was showing no sign of getting ready to halt, my father shot him. His head exploded and he tumbled from the bicycle, which miraculously kept careering towards the roadblock and even seemed to speed up, like an accidentally dismounted racehorse, until it crashed into the roadblock and disintegrated into its constituent pieces. My father ordered the pieces collected so that they might be used for currency.

A fortnight before the currency had been brown breadcrumbs. Ten days before that it was mobile phone skins, with pink ones holding the highest values and black ones the least. Then there had been a brief period when shoelaces ruled. I collected lettuce leaves with slugs on them, hoping that one day their turn would come and I would be rich. But I had forgotten to mention this to my father, which was a stupid mistake. My father now decreed that bicycle parts were the new currency of the estate and issued two further related decrees:

1) Establishing a five person currency committee to assign relative values to the different parts of bicycles.

2) Establishing a twenty-person provisions committee to sequester all bicycles and bicycle parts on the estate. This committee was also instructed to take food and hygiene supplies and anything else thought useful from all households on the estate which had not yet sent an able-bodied volunteer to take part in the roadblock and refused to send one now. This sub-decree was loudly and lengthily applauded.

After the currency committee had retired to their marquee and the provisions committee, suitably geared up, had headed off on their rounds, my father issued one further sub-decree:

3) Establishing himself as Governor of the Bicycle bank, and our next-door neighbour Mr Fixit in charge of the practical oversight of financial policy and affairs.

My father then announced, rather coyly, after clearing his throat, and rubbing his belly a little *I have composed an original air about the roadblock. A folksong for our times. An anthem for our cause. Perhaps.* Immediately the shout went up all around to hear it sung. My father said *I would be glad to oblige, very very glad, but I still have a little tweaking to do on the scansion and also wouldn't it better to wait until the provisions committee return*? All agreed it would be discourteous not to. *Let us set 18.30 hours for the performance, which we can put back if needs be to await the provisions committee. I promise a good show that all will enjoy. A damn good show.* It was my father's intention, obviously, to be be the poet-emperor of the roadblock, of our estate, and far beyond. Every tribe must have its songs to march along to.

However, at 18.00 an incredibly thick sea-mist rolled in, completely enshrouding the roadblock, reducing visibility to centimetres. No-one could see anything but shadows wandering round and looming through the mist. Occasionally their own dense images stared back at them out of the mist. It was so thick and indeed overwhelming that the shout of 'gas attack' went up. But that was not the case. Everyone could at least breathe, if damply, and the coughing we were hearing from the children's marquee was asthma surely. My father shouted for the arrest of the 'gas-attack provocateur' but no-one could see anyone else and no-one could tell who had shouted. In the mist my father had lost his surgical understanding of tactics. Like so many fathers before him, his great nemesis was the sea.

The sea, which is less than a mile from our estate, and can always be scented, and even viewed from certain vantage points, is a constant threat, sending sporing mists and blighting rains and shades and nightmares of the deep among us in our slumber hours. I have always felt that our estate—our entire continent in fact—is trespassing on the territory of the sea and that the sea's attitude towards us all is one of hateful lying-in-wait. Research tells that in our part of the coast, where we all walk about our airy little spaces, Anomalocaris of the metre-long teeth and the blazing eye-extensions ruled predatorily for millions of Cambrian years. In cosmic terms, we're barely dried out around here;

we still smell of salt and seagrass. And in the human era, how many shipwrecks and individual drownings within a few miles of us? So much death and terror floating around, (perhaps we are the Cambrian having a nightmare?) Is this what keeps us from reaching out to each other and from from mutual striving—the inner knowledge that we are but plankton in the churning sea of time? And the big whale called disaster casually drifting through our swarm, swallowing each one of us separately.

I often looked at my neighbours and tried to feel us all clamped together in a geological layer as we are bound to be, along with our houses and our cars and all of our machines and possessions. Everything of the last 16,000 years, since the dawn of agriculture and of urban man, will be a quarter centimetre of compacted muck turning to rock, or oil perhaps, miles down beneath the floor of future ocean. This ocean will likely teem with the ferocious descendants of whatever cunning, martial monster manages to outwit and outlast the asteroid-strike-equivalent known as humanity. That greater consciousness will know better than to ever again let life emerge from the sea into the demented theatre of the open air. It will flood the world entirely and freeze it over pole to pole with one hundred miles of ice. Clouds will drift eternally across the mirror of the world and all signals from the void will bounce.

Someone running in a panic to get away from the mist knocked me to the ground. Minutes later I was trampled, or kicked. I don't know which. A great clattering, a great round of aches, and then silence, numbness for a while.

When I came to my senses it was raining drearily but the mist had gone. My neighbours had all deserted the roadblock. The fair that had grown up around it had entirely emptied out. It was desolate, forlorn as only dead festivity can be. The generators still buzzed and hummed, machines of mockery. The whole belonged now to insects and to other scavengers, the ones who tidy up the world and recycle it. I shivered.

Metres away my father lay like an Elgin marble, broken and mutilated, his hacked limbs in disarray around him, his eyes gouged out. On his head there was a mustard-coloured paper crown, something from a lucky bag. On his naked chest someone had scrawled in lipstick or in his own blood perhaps the message THE KING IS DEAD LONG LIVE THE KING.

I sat down beside him and held out my hands, which looked like somebody else's, but they had looked like that for a long time.

The Cornerboy

Please come and visit. The most interesting thing about my village is The Cornerboy. He is celebrated even at a regional level. Although he has never set foot in any other village, close by or far away. No matter when you will come, you will see him. You must come soon. The Cornerboy is getting old and he is not eternal. Only one thing I must tell you is no photographs, video or audio recording is allowed. Please respect this. There are large fines for any breaches, which are always observed.

Every day The Cornerboy wears a different costume. Many of these will relate or refer to historical or legendary figures, or to figures from politics or the showbusiness world, or very often to figures from Art History. Greek, Roman, African, Chinese, Renaissance, Modernist and Postmodernist themes all show up from time to time. However, many times the costumes are completely original devices and difficult to contextualise. Sometimes, also, The Cornerboy will choose to be absurd and provocative. For example last Tuesday he wore nothing but goggles and a tie. But don't worry, most days his body is not in itself on display and, when it is, there are always signs erected on the approach to warn away children and the elderly and others who might be offended. You do not have cause to worry about anything in my village, which you must come and visit. His body in any case is not as offensive as most and has been described in the literature as *suitably sculptural.*

Very often large crowds come during high season coming to get a glimpse of The Cornerboy, who I will add was recently named in a list of the world's top 500 tourist attractions. When there are very large crowds each person or group of persons is issued with an electronic ticket, which expires after ten minutes. After fifteen minutes, if they have not left the zone of observation, the ticket, which is tagged at the ankle, emits a small shock. Every five minutes the shock increases in strength. My advice to you is, if you are nervous of crowds and especially if you are nervous of shocks, to come at low season, or in high season come very early on Sunday morning.

Most of my village's money goes on buying costumes for The Cornerboy. Everyone contributes what they can. We have six large warehouses full of clothes, props, and make-up. We have had to make alternative arrangements for the livestock, most of which we have in any case sold to stock the enormous wardrobe of The Cornerboy. But, you know, this is not a problem because now we all make money one way or another from the people who come and visit The Cornerboy, from souvenirs and food and hospitality and many other services. The morning (September 3rd thirty-two years ago) when The Cornerboy arrived at the north-eastern corner of the cross—some call it a star—at the heart of our village, to which he has returned every day without fail ever since, was the dawn of the modern in our village. We are not any longer desperate peasants whom one bad winter can annihilate. We are in business regular-style now, with stable credit lines. We can make plans for years in advance and be reasonably sure of achieving them. What remains completely and gloriously unpredictable is what The Cornerboy will be be wearing when he shows up today. That is known only to him, up until he orders his costume, which is normally about an hour before the display.

Some costumes are very elaborate and others quite simple. For example if The Cornerboy wishes to dress up as some kind of emperor or aristocrat or supermodel there is a lot of work in tailoring, make-up, sourcing materials and designs and so on. But if he wants to dress up as a slave or a prostitute all we have to do his hand him a tea towel, a length of chain and a dishrag.

It is true, and I admit this with shame and in the spirit of truthful atonement, that on the very first morning all those years ago, when The Cornerboy turned up dressed as a colourful hen, in a hen-suit he had obviously stolen from the marketing department of our local chicken factory, which up until then had been our main source of employment, income, and pride, that some locals, eager to defend the pristine reputation of our village throughout the region and beyond, began to throw mud, stones, and hard-boiled eggs at The Cornerboy. With luck, a visiting regional officer, here to inspect the progress on our then long ongoing and extremely controversial sewerage scheme, intervened. The regional officer, now a national principal officer, is a visionary man and has been instrumental in our village, our region and our nation's salvation in so many ways. He ordered that The Cornerboy be respected and furthermore treated as an asset, that he be allowed carry through his *wonderful experiment* without *molestation from the atavists.* Within a week, on the word of the regional officer, who had on his own initiative begun to speak to the regional press about The Cornerboy, cars and trucks and even buses began to come off the bypass and enter the town for a glimpse of The Cornerboy. Attitudes were soon transformed.

Many scientists and semioticians have come to study the costumes and, in particular, the sequences in which they are worn. They are trying to discover if the costumes do not form some kind of language which they can translate in order to discover the message or the messages The Cornerboy may be trying to express. But no such logic has so far been discovered. The Cornerboy may not in fact be trying to say anything. He may not wish to speak to us at all. The costumes are not ciphers, or letters, or runes in a 'costume language'. They are obviously not mating calls. But you will, I am sure, have your own theories about what The Cornerboy intends. You must come and visit.

The Cornerboy mostly stands upright with arms by his side, or else he slouches with pocketed hands. He sometimes introduces a performative element which enhances the display. He is fun-loving and mischievous and likes to work with contrast producing strange, hybrid effects, playing with cultural clichés and expectations. For example if he is dressed like a wolf he may baa like a sheep. He may shove a syringe in his right eyeball when dressed up as a nun. He is also musical and can play a bewildering variety of instruments, tunes and musical styles. One of his most famous displays, uniting many of these elements, has become known as The Dirty Harpist. The Cornerboy turned up, five years ago, mid-summer, Sunday, with hair and beard extension, smeared from head to foot in a mixture of animal excrements, including his own, with harp in tow, and proceeded to play dozens of tunes from the regional repertoire, many of them very obscure, and all of them given his own singular interpretation. Recordings of 'The Dirty Harpist' are available exclusively from our village musical store, along with dozens of other recordings representing the 'musical costumes' as they have become known to us. You must produce proof that you have gone to see The Cornerboy before you are allowed entry to the musical store.

I would like to emphasize that The Cornerboy is only occasionally sensational in this sense. Sperm, blood, vomit, shit, pus and urine rarely play a large part and, again, there will always be signs and warnings in place in order to avoid any possible upset.

You will perhaps read the rumour that the original Cornerboy, putatively a political troublemaker in open dispute with the Village Elders, was killed off long ago and replaced by an interchangeable battalion of Cornerboys appointed by the Village Elders. The Village Elders are accused of deciding the sequence and format of costumes *by committee* and *up to a decade in advance.* This is not true. If you met my village officers you would soon realise they know very little about costumes. A more baroque rumour accuses The Cornerboy of being a plot carried out by national government in league with international business concerns in order to test consumer sentiment regarding new styles and fashion accessories. Conspiracy theorists have gone so far as to suggest that The Cornerboy is a hologrammatic projection of an alien power known variously as 'The Spectacle' and 'The Mesmerists' and that everyone who goes to see The Cornerboy is nanotechnologically implanted with alien control devices. Another tale states that The Cornerboy does not exist and is in fact a mass hallucination created by mysterious powers of suggestion, which powers, by the by, ancient folklore ascribes to the people of my village and its environs. There are also many religious and pseudo-religious theories about The Cornerboy. All are completely unsubstantiated nonsense of course. However, the rumours generated by The Cornerboy are of great interest as a cultural phenomenon in themselves and have been collected into three separate volumes, which are available for purchase exclusively in our village and only after you have gone to see The Cornerboy. You must come and visit.

Of course The Cornerboy is not eternal and he will die. This is a problem for which there is no simple solution. I am one who supports memorialising The Cornerboy, as opposed to substituting him with a new Cornerboy or Cornerboys. I believe that people will not pay to see *an impression* of The Cornerboy. I also believe that if we in our village introduce the idea of *the Ersatz Cornerboy* then other villages will follow suit and what we will end up with is an economic collapse in my village, complete devastation. I am confident that our faction will win out in the end. The problem is how to memorialise such variegated and complex phenomena. How to find a form to represent in static posterity a dynamic that has taken so many forms, many of them basically irreconcilable and all of them irreducible to one another. We are really dealing with a counter-form, or an attempt to escape from form and this involves a basic antipathy to mediation, summary, reproduction, and, in a word, to memory itself.

There are two warring sub-factions within the memorialist faction. One supports the construction of an enormous 'Cornermuseum' on the site of the old chicken factory and surrounding farmland. The museum would somehow be made up of nothing but corners and points from which to view corners. There would be one corner for every single day of The Cornerboy's long run and each corner would contain an exact statuesque replica of an individual Cornerboy display. Now I know for a fact this will never come about, simply by applying some logic to the situation. The running total of Cornerboy displays now stands at 11659, and may reach 13, 14, or even 15 thousand by the time he passes away. The time it would take to exactly reproduce all these would be measured in years at least. Also, the money, not only to construct, but to maintain, staff and service such a museum would be beyond our national budget, not to mind local or regional. We would be paying through the nose for something we now not only get for free, but make vast profits from. The Cornermuseum is a cretinous folly dreamed up by economic illiterates. It will never see the light of day.

I am proposing a solution far more radical, original, inventive, attractive and financially beneficial to the members of our village community and our region as a whole, as well as one we can get off the ground as soon as The Cornerboy dies, with virtually no investment our end. It is this: We offer members of the public a chance to become The Cornerboy for a day—or an hour or even fifteen minutes at a time. We can work out a price structure and we can offer the potential Cornerboys the use of our vast Cornerboy stock from which to mix and match their own costume, or of course they can come up with one on their own. We can award weekly, monthly and annual *sponsored* prizes for Best Cornerboy. There is nothing but inflow to our ledgers and accounts and the village will be in an ongoing state of carnival and carnival is money. If we do this we will have turned The Cornerboy into a perpetual money machine and we will be able to live off The Cornerboy until Kingdom Come.

Do come and visit us and have a good old gander at our Cornerboy, truly one of the most amazing sights you will ever see. I must tell you however that if you do decide to come I will feel sorry for you as I feel sorry for all of our visitors; that they can only visit our wonderful village and not live here as I do and always have done, and always will, for the rest of my years, whatever there is to come in them.

The Iron Lady

When the Iron Lady died we melted her down immediately.

After some debate (coinage, medals, spearheads, an unique musical instrument, an elaborate candlestand…?) we decided to divide her and use her to make five Alloy Ladies.

These were the Cast Iron Lady, the Pig Iron Lady, the Celestium Lady, Lady Cobalt and the Lady of Ferrovanadium.

We placed an Alloy Lady on a special display pedestal at each one of our Starfort's five points and floodlit them from below. They were martial hallucinations, ethereal and terrifying.

The Alloy Ladies were taken by many of our citizens to be representations of cult deities; unofficial grottoes sprung up. These were always garlanded with fresh rose and hydrangea bouquets, perfumed with jasmine and incense, illumined by the flames of gigantic votive candles. Some citizens started leaving notes of supplication, as well as coins and other wish-offerings, but this was put a stop to as it was untidy, attracted petty criminals, and generated mendicancy.

The Alloy Ladies reminded one of our more mediocre blank verse poets of impressively-wrought ship's figureheads:

majesty at the prow
of a majestic vessel
guiding and protecting
remaining fixed and true
during every storm
during every threat
during every unforeseen
eventuality of the
unpredictable sea......

....continuing to lead
and to drive on the voyagers
no matter if it is for a Utopia
which will fulfil their
every fantasy the ship
is bound or whether the whole
crew and cargo will soon
be going over a bottomless
cliff at the edge of the world....

That was all besides the Alloy Ladies' principal message, to our enemies: Among us, death is only the Chieftain's latest political intrigue. It is a way of building strength and upgrading in secret, while at the same time drawing enemies into the open. It is a means of entrapment. The Great Ones among us simply step out of their old, exhausted bodies and into new and rejuvenated ones. They stay on top, in a new costume.

Centuries pass and fade and, although appearances change over and over again, the power of the Great Ones builds and builds, rooting and flowering in ever greater proportions and varieties, continuously increasing complexity and strength. Though they die a thousand times, our leaders are as indestructible as they are merciless.

Our enemies, ignorant of our true power, hear the rumours of the Iron Lady's passing. They have her apparent passing away confirmed by their frontier scouts and their informants. They march from every continental corner and set sail from every archipelago with their miserable conscripts and their ecstatic volunteers, with their grand stratagems to profit from the weakness and instability they mistakenly surmise as having taken hold of us in the aftermath of a head-of-state demise.

Inevitably, they will spy an Alloy Lady through far instruments and inevitably they will turn around and march back in the direction whence they came, embittered and disappointed, scurvy and rebellion coursing through their ranks.

We wait a week or so and then send forth the quartermaster's squadron to collect the enemy's abandoned horses and his wasted siege-engines. We do not often find deserters but when we do we interrogate them briefly and then we shoot them on the spot.

The demesnes approaching our Starfort are a confederation of decay, littered with deliquescing, rat-gnawed corpses, with sun-washed skeletons and stage-prop skulls. This obviously serves as another, perhaps even greater, warning to all our potential encroachers.

Innocence

But because thou art lukewarm, and neither cold, nor hot, I will begin to vomit thee out of my mouth. Revelation 3:16

So this fly lands on your forearm in the moonlight by the windowsill as you're spying over backyards and alleyways and thinking what's justice? What's justice to the fly? Heh? A field full of corpses at dawn. Or at the rising of the moon. Troy, Waterloo, Ypres, Ebro, Kursk, the Bulge, Inchon, Khe Sanh, Beirut, Najaf - a calendar of horrors to the human way of seeing, but to the fly a reel of Arcadias. You like to try and see things flyway, for the unburdening of it. You like to put on your flyface. Panning with your multiple ocelli across the heaps of twining limbs and spilling trunks, then swivelling in insect calculation across uprooted, carbonised tree-stumps, bubbling shell-holes, flaming hedgerows... then halting up to focus in on the somehow still upright hindquarters of a shrapnel-halved Friesian; but no, there's even more and better dining to be had, so you pan on hungrily again, dissatisfied yet, and trace the gut-bearing rivulets of blood and all loosed fluids you can think of as they are racing to oblivion in the lacerated earth. Then you pinpoint and zoom in on the well-fed body of a general or upon the fragmented, exposed anatomy of a lance corporal, all rankings being irrelevant and inappropriate to your ravenously democratic appetite. Your banquet awaits you. You are an aristocrat of death. You'll feast on flesh and blood until you're drunk with it and fit to burst.

Oh if a fly could shriek, and maybe it can, in some unbearable frequency beyond our hearing, it would be shrieking now, it would shriek and shriek and shriek with glee, shrouded there, while hovering, in the flavoursome mists of the aftermath, inhaling the meatstink of this carnally marvellous moonlit morning, then buzzing onward to land on a choice, still-pumping shank, or on a slivered rump.

When the dead are a multitude, uncovered and fresh, that's when the fly gets its fulfillment, the grade A rot it has been longing for, allitsbriefexistence longing for.

Nice...ummmm...sweet...delicious...the fly thinks when it lands and pads itself into something freshly deadandgone. Of course you don't have to tell yourself that flies don't actually think. They feel. They sense. They compute. Take this one right here, right now, this little machine of survival crawling around in the congeals of your sweat and stink, crawling around in the tastes and vapours of another burnt down day.

You admit that you sometimes meander, like a drunken idiot with none or too many responsibilities. Staccato nonsense leading towards a greater ignorance. But for sure, the mainframe is sound. All your faculties remain under central control. You are logical. You comprehend. You know where you are. You know what moves you have to make to stay in the game. You can connect sensation to thought, thought to deed, quick and rational. You just yabber on like this now and then, when you get excited. When the topic upsets you. When the action-point approaches. You sweat, palpitate. Swift, irregular, agitated breaths. You twitch and shudder unpredictably. Your elbows, for example, they twitch. And your cheeks too. You have to piss a lot. Nervous jolts interrupt your flow of thought. You have read that the same kind of complex affects actors and other performers in the hours before they go on stage. You have that much in common with Madonna and Marlon Brando. In any case, you can't help your natural vulnerability to agitation. In fact, you don't wish to. The relief when you get the damn thing you have to do done is more than compensation. A plateau of calm, self-satisfied glory ensues, and it lasts, and lasts, as if nothing in the world had any harm or consequence in it, as if all the previous worry had never been.

Achievement is a way we have of flattening the past. EAT! Eat the Fucking Universe, says you. It's all food to the fly, sticking out his sucker pad, the shape and length of it unavoidably calling to mind a medieval battle horn. That carrion clarion. Sup. Sup. Sup. Sup by sup it disappears you. You're disappearing, into a fly. You can see a patch of sea from your window too. *Inspiring Seascapes* is what the brochure said, selling the place to you. The brine's a mile off. Two miles maybe. Can't see it in the night directly, only infer it from the thickness, the darklustre of the grape-dense shade between the far rows of houses. Yet it will be flagrant under the sun in the morning, streaked in fragile pink or perhaps splashed in that blood-bright red that is nature's high tribute to the planet of slaughter underneath. That's if there is a sunrise—which you predict there will be. Absolutely everything depends, from the minutest to the most enormous, upon the continuing fulfillment of our simplest prophecies.

Just as it did so long long ago for Ptolemy. Ptolemy!

The sea. The poison-slurping shit-eating sea. What's justice for the sea? Sink or swim. Isn't that it? Drown or drift along with the prevailing current whichever way it's headed. So at 4am, with precision, (what a jagged term that is—precision!)

the window at 234 will be broken. The glass will shatter. And the noise of it in dreams or semi-wakeful state to the neighbours could be both beautiful and terrifying. Mellifluous before association. If we could just break sounds from the origin or the consequence we could eclipse the terror altogether. Do not tell yourself that you do not find the undulating whine of shells on a war documentary a musical treat for your ears. Everything is music. Isn't that the radical viewpoint? Once we don't get too emotional about it. Ensconced on your settee, following the screened projections of faraway crosshairs, you are thrilled in a zone down there below your bellybutton by the anticipation of that colossal thump and almighty levelling when the bomb or the missile cracks home. Armies have always had music at their command. You wouldn't be surprised if they invented it. That martial brass and thunder on the march, that trumpeting into the charge. Pianos in the deathcamps. Humonsters will do anything to a melody.

Smashglass on a housing estate sound is always clear and gorgeous. It is music, no matter what. It is a sound that initiates so many imaginings, opening into some secret narration of the shattered and abused among the elements. Is it not? Or it is just meaningless, if you like. Please yourself. But for you there is no such strict segregation between terror and beauty. War in your ear is beautiful because it is terrible. You do not seek, nor need, distraction from the deed at hand. Murder sings most lyrical and eloquent to you. The window breaks and you nod your head in agreement, appreciation. Because you have predicted it. It is so because you have said it. You are both king and minion of this *evenement*, this local cataclysm, sponsored by yourself.

There were too many dogs on your estate. Big dogs. Shitting everywhere. Bloodthirsty bastards every one of them. Eyeing up toddlers for the inevitable. You have a procedure for big leashless dogs. In the first place you approach the person or persons you assume to be the proprietor(s) of the dog(s) and inform them, with an affect of extreme courtesy, that they are legally obliged to have their animals under control at all times. This elicits a variety of responses. Nervous types immediately conform and give assurances to keep their big dog leashed at all times while using the public, that is not quite public, let's say the locally-shared and utilised parts of the common estate. Some others grunt begrudging assent or swear violent oaths against you. You never respond in kind. You are far too weak in the physical sense for that. You just walk off smirking, your invisible tail cocked and aimed in stiff hatred, like a duelling sword sticking out of your arse. Now, as for stage two of your procedure, kicking in when you spot a dog roving unleashed in the demesne for a second time, you phone the Guards. The Guards always tell you to ring the dog warden. The dog warden never answers her phone. You doubt if there is a dog warden. Public services are being replaced by pre-recorded messages. These are DIY days we live in for sure. If you want a job done then off you go and DIY my son. Pull your own teeth, lance your own sores, saw off your own gangrenous feet. So, to stage three—laying poison on the green. In the dark, and watch out for the traitorous moonlight. Within a day or so the dog is dead. And has died off horribly, shitfarting its intestines, puking up its heart and lungs, screeching in an almost human terror. The pain is so intense it almost causes speech in dogs. Very very upsetting for the owners, and if there are children in the house...well it's terrific. All the vet can do is needle the mutts into eternity. Six of the biggest are down now - three Rottweilers, two German Shepherds, and a Doberman pup.

Are you a suspect? Well of course. But many others are too. And dog serial killers are among the many kinds of criminals the Guards do not investigate. A lot of people moan about the dogs. Some complain directly to the owners or the Guards like you do. To cover yourself further, before you kicked off your campaign you spoke at length about the mutt issue to the management company and to the local free paper. The management company routinely sent out a letter headed DOG CONTROL ISSUES. The 'paper' printed your comments verbatim, without mentioning you, as requested. Anonymous, official printed words have an absolving quality for you.

So, smithereening glass. You can't wait to hear it. That song of the broken. Crying out in grief and rage for restitution. A feudsound.

Feuds, these days, in our kinds of societies, as everyone truly candid will admit, are a kind of social hygiene. Feuds dispose of a certain otherwise potentially costly portion of the hopeless, the ones that can't be either retrained or restrained, who are completely lacking in self-discipline and self-esteem, and are impossible therefore to profitably exploit. But these feuding losers are endlessly useful as an ideological object lesson for those clinging to the rungs above them (*this is where you are going drudge if you don't submit*) as they consume themselves in bloody in-fighting, and kill off the costliest male recidivists. Extremely efficient and blameless way of doing it, isn't it?

You are very lucky in your country, to have an indigenous and self-reproducing scapegoat.

You don't want to be a hero. You only want to take revenge. On none in particular, and everyone in general. On the living. On the most convenient among the living in your vicinity.

All you are doing is accelerating, oh so very slightly, the process of decay—you might declare it, more positively, transformation—already decided and well under way and out of your hands completely. You are not really changing anything.

Global statistics will be totally unaffected.

There are two families, large, extended families. Interrelated partially through all kinds of secret and shameful violations. They all look alike anyway. The way you look at them. Mirror images of each other. The children of a nameless, sourceless, unquenchable hate. Yes, a murderous hatred is the law and the father of them all, sire of every one of their bastards. A mutual murderous hatred that goes back decades, even centuries... God knows, but time is not its true dimension. Their hate is a numbersmashing clockderanging gale from beyond time; it blasts across time and destroys it. Calendars and dates have no effect on this hate—they go to shreds before it. This hate has nothing to do with history and society either. However, to those whom it produces and consumes, this hatred is history and society. Hatred is their universe, their matter.

So there is much less prep work to do than with the dogs. Everyone around here is already itching to be rid of these overbreeding pricks already, and nobody will be blamed only themselves. No press. No Guards. No wardens. No rumourstarting needed either. Their presence, in our context, causes rumours of its own accord.

The haterage of the roadless, boxed-in nomad is in a parellel to that of the commonnogarden entowered urban greaselump punching through walls and kicking in televisions at random times of the day and night, and also beside the rural and perirural poppyheads who box each other braindead in pukegardens and crossroads pubs all over Ireland every weekend. This haterage has a grotesque, mythical quality. It is a pure explosive passion that is not even animal. It has to do with the days before the animal and the vegetable and the mineral. It is a preserve of the days of spewing formation. The billion year days and millisecond centuries of cosmic bangs and pregalactic conflagrations.

You have just had a thought: what if the cosmos is God's vomit?

You think of your close neighbours' mutual detestation as a two-headed dog, a Cerberus that has turned upon itself. Both heads hating each other unto death. Both dog heads ready to snap, tear and crunch and rip the life out of the other one at the first excuse and opportunity.

All you are doing is removing the muzzle.

You will use an ould device to get those muzzles off. One from the national stock of devices. Tonight at 4am you'll feck a petrol bomb through the downstairs window of 234. You won't be caught. The residents of 234 will surely all be sleeping after the evening's feed of drink. Everyone else around will have their doors all shut and their windows blinded, such is the feudfear now soaking the neighbourhood. And behind the blinds most will no doubt be cosydozing under the influence of one or other form of legal sedation. Unwakeable by any means. An Elysian tranquility.

Now, either the resulting blaze will burn all at 234 to death—yippee!—or else they will totally or partially survive it. In the first case the other feuding household will take the rap. At the very least the clamour for *their* removal will force the council and the Guards to re-resettle them away from here. Local pleasantness and equilbrium restored. Hurray! In the event of survivors, frenzied acts of vengeance against the other household will immediately commence, resulting, one fervently wishes, in more deaths, serious injuries, arrests and long-term incarcerations. In short, the mutually assured destruction of the contending asses.

And not much of a press fuss about it either. These people often go missing for long stretches, their babies and infants suffer 'cot deaths' at ten times the going rate, their children are gang-raped in laneways and bogs, their women are so badly beaten that their faces are nothing but scab and black bruise, none of which is found the least bit troubling in good neighbourhoods like yours.

Not at all. Ye had a murder a few months back, the one that sparked the latest episode of feud, and the local paper—the one that gives prominent coverage to Under 14 rugby and the goings on at local table quizzes—held their nerve admirably and didn't mention a word about it. *Fair play to them,* wrote Neighbour No 1 on boards.ie, *isn't it bad enough trying to sell a house around here without broadcasting the carry on of that lot?*

The fly. The fly is silent. Perhaps it has died on you.

What time is it?

Exactly, what time is it now?

A Bone

One day, or night, a man arrived in to me carrying a bone. The bone was a large knee joint, as would befit the leg of a cow or a horse. But it belonged to neither of those. I did not recognise the animal of origin, and I do not like to guess. The light was as poor as it usually is where I am standing, so how could anything be defined and categorized with any confidence? To tell you the truth, this once, I was not troubled. It was a bone. That was all. It would do. I did not recognise the man either. He didn't belong to our group. But so what? Members of other groups often drop by without any hostile intentions, and they sometimes approach me with an offering for the stew, thinking to get some stew for themselves in return. You may be sure, if they have come to see me, and they are carrying a bone, they are hungry.

You may believe a bone to be a poor offering but it is not. Bones are brittle honeycombs at the core of every animal. They are the base ingredient of any decent stock, stew, soup or broth. So much flavour is held in the marrow of every bone, awaiting heat and a pot and a cook to release it.

Having said all that, of course it's not possible to accept any old bone, from any old hand. Each ingredient for the stew, bone or no, must be properly inspected and found free of all threats and defects.

I am the person in our group with sole responsibility for the stew. I have to stir it, all day long. I have to ensure it is evenly and continuously heated. I have to add ingredients, with all necessary prudence, as they become available to me. I have to proportionately distribute the stew to the members of my group, and occasionally to members of other groups who, for one reason or another, find themselves in our location.

Distribution of the stew is a complex affair. It must take place according to custom and practice, of which, by custom and practice, I am the interpreter. But also according to need. The hungriest has gained a certain priority. They have often done the most work, whether or not they have been successful. But not the fattest. I do not feed according to girth.

Lastly, I do have to take merit into account. It is possible to deserve more or less than the average helping of stew. I am the agreed and only judge of this desert. I would say I try to be objective but that would be obvious gibberish.

As you can imagine, my position as the Stew Custodian, a position I have held for quite some time now, means I have a great deal of influence and power within the group. But it also makes me feel very vulnerable and nervous. Bacteria can run riot anytime. So, anyone could accuse me of poisoning them. In a week of thin stew, when hunger gnaws away like saw teeth at the tensing bonds of our mutuality, many tempers can flare simultaneously. A catastrophic riot is not an unlikely event. This, by the way, is how I came to be guardian of the stew. Hunger is the great catalyst in human affairs. I am not sure anyone but me remembers the previous Guard, his awful grimace when I skewered him. This group is not given to remembering. I have belonged to other groups who were obsessed with record, ritual and recall. But in this current group there are no record keepers. We do not speak to each other of our yesterdays. There are no rituals or customs to speak of outside of those to do with the stew, and these are not ornate. The stew consumes our energies and satisfies our wants. That is its purpose of course. We hunt therefore we eat. We eat therefore we hunt. We stir the stew and the stew stirs us.

So far then, I have not been seriously challenged for the stew. The overarching reason for this is simple: the power vested in me by the group to ration or even entirely deny the stew to offenders against the stew. If you offend me, you offend the stew. If you offend the stew you offend our entire group, simultaneously. The offence multiplies among us until it becomes capital. It is not taken lightly. So far, in the heart of each individual member of our group, and in their collective heart, the fear of not getting any stew at all has prevailed over the desire to win control of the stew.

*

I pass the time childishly, as if there were right and wrong, by imagining myself in certain pantomime roles. The wicked witch or conniving wizard. The pirate cook in the south sea galley. A vicious washerwoman in a fairytale from the black woods. A dubious prophet or prophetess stirring the stew as if the stew were time itself, full of whirling meat and scraps.

It is also true that the consistent and regular stirring motion and noise are conducive to trance like states and hallucinations, to which I have never been averse in first place. I can retain certain lucid leverage over these stew visions, or I can let go and see what happens. The one danger is falling into the stew, which would ruin both it, and me. I seem to instinctively know when this is about to happen and to snap myself aware again.

Lucidly, my favourite stewdream is to watch the faces of old friends and relations rise up to the surface of the stew and bob and revolve a while there, each in their turn. They are always clean shaven and I like them to have their mouths open so I can look down into them. I have always found looking down into people's mouths a great distraction. There may be a gold tooth to be spied, gaps and fillings, or a tongue that unfurls into a dragon.

When I let the stew take over anything can happen, as in dreams. A child visits an elderly lady on her death bed. White linen everywhere. I mean the bed, the room, the child, even the old woman are all made of white linen.

*

Onions, of course. Root vegetables. Salt and pepper —strictly rationed, meticulously apportioned. Meat: various beasts, various cuts. Nettles. Dandelions. Berries. Mushrooms and toadstools. Toads. Lilypads. Whatever can be picked, plucked, gathered, murdered, salvaged. Almost everything still abroad and edible finds its way into our stew.

*

Sometimes they are not faces of the people traipsing down the long tracts of my memory that I conjure up in the stew, but faces of stars and planets and comets that I have invented and can busy myself in naming and forgetting.

*

Where did you get the bone?
I found it.
You were alone?
Yes.
Far from here?
Not far.
And the rest of the beast?
No idea.
What was it?
No idea.
Some new animal?
Perhaps. Perhaps it was a new kind of man.
Hardly.
Or an old kind we haven't heard of. There used to be so many kinds. Long ago.
Really. You know so much.

It is a bone. That's all I know.
Bring it over here.
It's yours.
It's as smooth as a basin. You have picked it clean.
That was how I found it.
Open your mouth.
What?
Your mouth!
(He opens his mouth.)
You have kept all your teeth.
And no one else's.
You know someone who wears another person's teeth?
I know of no such. But I can imagine it.
I have heard it is done. I knew a man once who wore a crown of ears. He had subjected them to some process. They were as hard as marble, and glistened like it too.
The bone?
Yes?
Have you a use for it in the stew?
I'm not sure. It has so little perfume to it.
Because it is clean, and fresh.
You think it has any flavour?
More than likely, yes.
I prefer them to be older.
Well, lay it by then.
But the stew is losing substance.
Then use it immediately.

You are too quick to find solutions.
Excuse me.
I prefer not to solve things so quickly.
It is easier that way. Never solve one problem until you have another one ready.
Without obstacles I would malfunction.
How do you avoid it?
I just put things off and keep stirring. Time passes, without a resolution.
What do you make of time?
It is an infinite womb.
Or a birth canal from which there is no exit.
What's inside it never truly sees the light.
You're optimistic.
Imagine the void that awaits us at the end of our troubles.
Imagine. I can't. Impossible.
We should have no excuses left then.
At the end of our appetites.
There would simply be new appetites, new senses, new lusts upon us.
If only hunger and lust could both be satisfied with the one bite.
That doesn't add up. Hunger ingests, lust expels. Sex is a kind of excretion.
I can't argue with that. I thought that up myself, ages hence.
I'm getting mixed up. Did we decide to put the bone in or not?

We hadn't decided.
I'm putting it in. I might as well. There.
It bubbles.
It hisses.
It whistles.
It yabbers.
Do you think it is trying to speak?
Yes, like all things.
What is is it trying to say?
It is trying to say thank you, to pay tribute, surely.
To what? To whom?
To us both, and, for allowing it to speak, to the stew, most of all to that.
Let's join it then.
Let's toast. Your cup?
I thought I might take a sip from yours.
I sip from the ladle.
You drip-feed yourself?
I do.
You won't share?
I can't.
There is only one solution.
There is a solution? Don't terrify me.
I will enter the stew.
You will not.
I will.
(With that the second, unrecognised man leaps into the pot and disappears whistling and bubbling beneath the steam).

*

Because I do not sleep while I am stirring the stew does not mean I do not dream or wake up from my dream in which there is an almostcorpse. A person who has suffered some terrific mishap and is now lying unconscious in a private room in an ultra hi-tech hospital attached to complicated and impressive life support machinery.

This near-death individual does not know where they are nor what has happened them to be in such a state. In fact, when he or she occasionally opens his or her eyes it is always to a slightly different gleaming room with slightly different gleaming machinery keeping him or her alive. Perhaps he or she is in a different room on a different floor or ward, or in a different hospital altogether each time.

Varying levels of insurance cover are implied, and even different incidents or accidents as the cause of the hospitalisation.

*

Was it fields that gave war its start? I mean, how could there be war without fields?

Attacks on the House

*****

The motorcyclists were the first to attack, just as it was getting dark, just as the bats were beginning to whirl out of their daytime redoubts in the woods, diving and wheeling like Stukas in the grounds. Often, in the past, when things had been different, a bat had flown in through a window or a door or a vent. On occasion this had seriously spooked one of the residents, whose hypersensitive artistic imaginations could work against them, leading to complaints and even refunds. These days, under new management, a bat in the house was a rare event. Precautionary measures included:

1) Chicken wire over all vents, which also prevented the entry of other pests, but not insects or spirits of course.

2) Signage on all the doors clearly instructing staff, residents, and visitors to SHUT THE DOOR TO PREVENT THE ENTRY OF UNWANTED GUESTS OF ALL KINDS

3) Strict, regular and continuous instruction to all staff, residents, visitors, occasional workmen and guests by members of the management sub-

committee tasked with ensuring that only those people and things got into the house that were officially allowed into it.

The bikers all wore similar parched and dusty leathers, insignia and helmets. I remember best of all the blood red lightning flash sewn into the upper right arm of their padded jackets. A martial gang, no doubt about it. Hunnish, I decided. Approaching in a crescendo of deafening noise, completely drowning out our conversations. Everybody noticed the noise but I was the only one to understand from the very beginning that this was an attack and not an unremarkable convoy of hobbyists on an outing merely passing through the grounds. All the residents, myself among them, were already in the drawing room, having dined and conversed around the long table and afterwards collectively tidied up in the kitchen. We were by this time well settled into our usual evening congregation. A very sedate evening as usual. Languid small-talk, soft-voiced preludes to our oncoming dreams. A wind-down, with wine and digestives. We had as usual been discussing how work on our various artistic projects had gone during the day, before moving on to the house, its histories and traditions, such as who had been raped here, who among the staff had systematically pilfered from the stock, who among present and past guests had been haunted, in which rooms they had been haunted, and by whom they had been haunted. The shift from narcissism to scandal was seamless as always.

But now everything in the drawing room shook as if in terror/worship of the engine God; the antique furniture shook, the sub-standard art that previous guests had left behind on the walls as gifts or payments-in-kind shook, the hundred year old Blackwood's Almanacs and Punch Magazine annuals shook in shaking cabinets. Our teeth and bones shook. We couldn't hear ourselves think. We couldn't hear each other even if we shouted as loud as we could. We were reduced to rudimentary sign languages and trying to read each other's humours and intentions through the hues and tics passing over our faces.

The most terrified of all was a poet and mystical healer who had never published and was not intending to. In an attic room notorious for its poltergeists and malevolent presences she had been haunted by Nazis in league with 'an entity of pure evil'. Fortunately, she had at the last moment been saved by three benign ghosts from different generations of the colonials who had once owned the house along with its extensive holdings of forestry and farmland. In the past every one of the guests had paranormal encounters like this, she said, but now there was only herself, and maybe one or two others. I tried to sign the following to her, although I did not succeed: *the motorbike has a Nazi soul, just like the helicopter is a scalping Yankee.*

*****

After hours and hours of sonic aggression the motorcyclists retreated, having presumably run out of fuel. But that was not the end of it. Next, from all directions, the so-called North Vietnamese attacked. But I was not surprised. The Ulster hills and the monsoon weather had implied their imminence. War is like lymphatic cancer. It spreads to everywhere eventually, no matter where it starts off, even if it takes dozens of years. The American war had been traveling through the underground veins of the world for thirty years and now it had decided to erupt here in front of us. That was all. I had also befriended a young Texan who had had his cock and balls blown off near Saigon and was now living in the boathouse trying to figure things out. Experimental weapons, based on insane doses of electricity, he told me, had affected a mass transfer from 1971 through to now-here. The NVA now-here in Drumland, (pastiching the enemy, defeating the Yanks and the Aussies by copying and exceeding their depravity), had taken to decorating themselves with the body parts of the slain. One elephantine beauty had made himself a lovely dangling trunk out of a couple of dozen stitched together penises. Others had also decorated their helmets beautifully with shorn penises, transforming the helmets into sacrilegious crowns by attaching a ring of flopping cocks, black, white and mulatto.

*****

The house was attacked by porn stars. But is 'stars' the correct term? *He whose face gives no light shall never become a star*. Stars are extremely common and innumerable in the universe. And, what's more important, by the the time you get close enough to touch them they aren't even there anymore. The stars look at us and we look at them and both looks contain the knowledge of the impassable abyss between us. I recognised all the attacking stars of course. They were all the porn stars I had jerked off to since the internet. A true legion. A swarm. A large and twirling galaxy with a super massive blackhole in the middle of sucking and sucking and swallowing every thing. Big Bukkake Galaxy. Not that the stars were all the same but interchangeable they certainly were. Internet Masturbation helps me understand the fundamentally split being of, say, the genuine Franciscan. As his to any Magdalene, my inclinations towards the women of pornography are both pastoral and perverse. Perverse before orgasm, pastoral after. That is the best I can do. That was what I confessed to Helen, who had travelled all over and been the cause of some arguments, and she was OK about it. The porn stars ran right up to the bay windows and then they turned into moths, hideous insects with beautiful wings flickering for a while before heading back into the night with no beginning or end to it.

*****

Meanwhile one gets used to living under siege. Is there any other kind of living? This big house had been built, like all dwelling places, to withstand siege, siege from the elements, siege from the animals, siege from human and even supernatural enemies. Everything among the living and the dead is under siege, withstanding siege. Every shape is a siege shape. The planet bombarded by asteroids for a billion years, the asteroids bombarded all the time by cosmic rays, the cosmic rays bombarded by time, and time bombarded by something else we haven't found out about yet.

*****

In the drawing room, the literary-artistic conversation had moved on to technique. Everyone is getting a little obsessed with technique, I stated, and all seemed in agreement, or at least they did not openly disagree. When people have nothing to say, or think you have nothing to say, when they are without passion for anything at all and think that you are just the same, they want to talk to you and interrogate you about technique. But technique is only paranoia with a plan, I said.

*****

Hares attacked the house. Suicidally. They bounded out of the undergrowth at the far end of the garden and, when they got close enough, leapt at the bay windows, perhaps with the idea of breaking through, who knows, but only succeeding in pulverising themselves, in thudding themselves dead or deeply unconscious, the way whole flocks of birds are wont to do, rousing disturbing suspicions of the possibility of mass suicide in animal species. Animals are not supposed to know that they are going to die, that they can choose to die at any moment. *Animals are in the world like water in water.* Hares are magical animals in some people's minds. In some people's minds they leap down from the moon. And if they can leap down from the moon they surely can kill themselves. Soon after basset hounds, cute and murderous, came into view and started to feast on the fallen hares. Then riders arrived in the picture, in chase of the hounds. After these, death came with his big green sack, taking his time but gathering everything. And then the hares, the hares again, the hares came bounding after death, though they must have known they would never catch it, for if they did, what would happen? Life would exponentially explode and the universe would soon become so crowded with creatures not one of them would have any room to move. I began to doubt that this was an attack at all, but some kind of lesson intended to display the fundamental importance of death to peace and stability in the universe. But why would death need propaganda? Why would death need to start teaching lessons all of a sudden? What was death worried about? I asked my colleagues but they didn't have a clue though one was painting crows, real crows that at the same time were omens of doom, she said. I told her that in the art of crows, in the pictures painted by crows and in the sculptures chiseled out of coal and obsidian by crows, the human being is a symbol of birth canals and plenitude but also of stupidity and waste.

*****

The house was attacked by envious students from our various creative writing and life drawing classes. All our successes should have been their success. All our praises should have been their praises. All our invites and prizes should have been their invites and prizes. The jealous, accusing students attacked and attacked but they really had nothing to attack us with. They were nothing only steam and pus without us. We had given them all their ideas and inspiration. Of course they wanted to learn but they wanted most of all to replace us in the scholar's chair, to be the master in the comfortable seat, to be the one with all the ready-made answers. Or else they mistook us for the ones who had caused their deepest wound and transferred all that repressed bile and hatred unto us. I saw my own most jealous student out there howling in the grounds and I knew be the cut of her just what she had reduced her thinking down to: the book I was writing was really her book, the high literary life I was living was really her high literary life. Even these sentences right here belonged to her. I had stolen all my lines, good and bad, from her. These thoughts irritated me. Her presence in my field of vision irritated me so I rubbed her out, bit by bit. I rubbed the left side of her face, and then her complete midriff, and then her right foot, and then the backs of her knees. I rubbed her out inch by inch until the space where she used to exist was as blank as a freshly laundered sheet.

Living in IKEA

So, babes, when are you planning to come and live with me here in IKEA?

I've said it before, IKEA is a great place to live; it's as big as an asteroid; it takes a whole four hours to walk around. Stock rotation is constant. By the time you get back to where you started, the product display is bound to have changed. There's always some interesting new thing to stop at and fiddle with. There's a different chair to sit on, a different bed to lie on, a different bowl to spoon from for every day of your life, even if you lived here for a century.

The catalogues are very regularly refreshed and I feel that what I read in them is the quality equivalent, in terms of both stimulating imaginative literature and hard information, with what you'd find in any any bookshop or library.

Time doesn't really seem to pass in here, though motion is constant. I feel younger, sleeker, more alert. Maybe it's the air conditioning, which is science at its steady-stating best; it's always cool and comfortable in here. Maybe it's because the people who come here are generally more serious and mature in their pursuits than elsewhere I have shacked up. Which suits my long-term outlook now; I don't want to spend the rest of my days mall-hopping and I really feel IKEA is going to last for all the decades that I'm going to need. I can't say that about where you are.

You love people-watching; you should come and watch the people in IKEA. You should see the endless procession of faces beatifically aglow in the light engineered to add aura to the merchandise. It seems as if everything is in a painting by Tintoretto, or some other Venetian.

Imagine the people making their luminous passage from morning till night, beginning at the automatic entrances, then up the aisles, pausing, down the aisles, pausing, examining things, pausing, discussing things, pausing, comparing things, pausing, selecting things, pausing, buying things and then finally automatically away out through the entrances again with their purchases.

Imagine the talking all of the time, the millions of words, whole dictionaries of words spilling from thousands of mouths, all indecipherable due to the vaulting, cathedralesque acoustics in here. No one is able to clearly hear anyone but the closest, and I am never close enough to hear a single word. The rest is murmur, ceaseless, the best I've ever heard, such texture, such depth, so relaxing, so babble-therapy. Like a white noise jacuzzi.

High above, the roof, our great canopy of silence, receives the breathy updrafts and quashes every muddled decibel.

The only clarity lies in the orders issued over the intercom in a stern Nordic-inflected monotone. I love these too, since they arrive a little unpredictably and break the prayerful atmosphere somewhat, and also because they allow me to fantasise that I am in some enormous Belle Epoque train station, searching for my international platform.

It's amusing to try and lipread, and I'm getting good at it. You know how much of an autodidact I can be when I put my mind to it. The other day, from a distance of 200 metres away, across the sofa display, I read a woman saying to a man, *I'm not going to the Abbey theatre. I'm going to stand outside on Talbot Street, clapping the junkies instead.* I read a little boy saying, *If you don't get me chocolate I'm going to burn the house down tonight while you're sleeping.* I read a wheelchair-bound old lady self-whispering, *I have committed grave evils, which I don't remember precisely and this makes me very sad, and very happy, oh Lord.* I have also observed people laughing uncontrollably, weeping uncontrollably, vomiting, having seizures, and even brawling and being professionally excluded from the premises. There are many small accidents—there is a nurse on duty—and the occasional handbag robbery. I am sure there will be a murder eventually, and that waters will break here. Certainly conception has occurred. Did you ever think about your conception? Mine was in North London, against an alleyway wall, and they were both drunk. If either of them had slipped before the finish I'd have dripped like snot or snail-gunge down the wall and ended up a rat's aperitif.

Never the sun but always the eye candy, always something gamey to gawk at in IKEA, staff or client. Thank heaven for the space, the privacy, and the hygiene supplies in the toilets. I won't go into the details (or will I?). You know I still need you in so many ways.

My diet's going well. The lack of variety in the restaurant is a real help. The meat-balls (balls-meat I call 'em!) are always the same; cheap and fortified with zinc and molybdenum. They keep you alive, and satisfied. I down them as a last resort, when I am starving.

Sometimes a person stops before a just-posted temporary sign containing the revised small print of a special offer on a standard three-piece-suite with corner unit and they are so hushed and furrowed it is as if they have found the location of their stillborn twin on a map of limbo, or a detailed description of the very worst things that will happen to their descendants for all of the next five thousand years.

I know coming here was a risk and I do feel something of a pioneer but it's not that big a deal actually. Actually, I get the intuition on occasion that a good percentage of the 'passing trade' are only pretending as I am and are in fact living here as well. I mean, like whole families; that would be something new, no doubt about it. I mean, where would we have left to go then? But how could you tell? About if they are really living here I mean. You'd need access to the CCTV system. Which, btw, is a giant bluff here just the same as it is where you are. Up there, in the central security room, the dudes with the fancy earpieces and the blue lightning tattoos and the stun-guns are either too stoned or they're playing Halo or they're simply proto-simian to begin with, as is always the case. You will appreciate how lonely it is when you're not being watched or hunted. It's like you're sitting in shadow beside a parent in a coma waiting for them to speak and bring you both back. Or it's like an ancient companion who's refusing to acknowledge you for some dark reason neither of you will admit.

Normally, you see, crime is a kind of ongoing dialogue between the law and the criminal. There's back and forth, to and fro, action and reaction, and that's how the story keeps going and the plot is developed. There's a promise eventually of some kind of climax that you and the law are both advancing towards in mutual dependency. Around here, there's no such exchange. The hunters are so absent that I don't ever feel I'm committing any wrong by being here, under so-called false premises. Of course I miss feeling guilty, and of course I have never felt so much that my premises are true ones as I do here in IKEA. Three months and I haven't had one odd look from any kind of staff. Truth is, I blend in so well that no one notices me much, which can get kind of lonely, and I can get cranky with it, but it also means that I can do whatever I want to do and be whoever I want to be. I've never felt so in charge of myself, and at the same time so spontaneous, as I have since moving to IKEA.

It's boring being a customer all the time. Sometimes I pretend to be a security guard and I stalk—it's kind of kinky—and sometimes when I get a mania for counting things I'm a stock control guy. These are my three basic role-plays. OCD and boring as ever, I know.

On the other leg, and this might piss you off, but I'm in lust with one of the Mauritian waitresses in the restaurant. She has permanently bloodshot eyes from I don't know what (let's be honest, I fantasise that it's from all night fucking on the purest cocaine) and a diamond stud in her nose which is a bit tarty and doesn't suit her imho. She also has lips that seem browner than her skin, which I find fascinating. Whenever she is here serving balls-meat for €2.50 a tray I hang around discreetly and, as if I were an old-fashioned clock on the restaurant wall, I watch her merciless hours on this earth passing by, tick by unrelenting tick.

I'm a bit tired now. I can't get a flow going here. Every paragraph I write seems to be written by a totally different person, or by a different part of me at least. Is that a ridiculous thing to admit? Doesn't everybody feel like that, at least some of the time? Whenever they halt up and attempt to observe themselves in process, as it were, for a while? I don't know. I haven't slept for a month or something. My eyes are all webby. I saw a goat in the wardrobe section a half an hour ago. Right now, I'm hearing a seal bark—hoarse, high-pitched, hysterical—from the coffee aisle.

Now, before I sign off for a jaunt through the garden furniture, how are things panning out in Dundrum?

I don't know how you can stick it for such a long unbroken stretch over there, especially after the floods. I'll never get rid of the sight of all those floating mannequins. They looked so terribly pious and affronted, a congregation of the front-pew faithful after being water-cannoned by the altar boys.

There'll be no floods here though. The Swedes are not as frigging corrupt or cyclops-stupid as our crowd. Or they are stupid and corrupt on a higher plane than our crowd. Is it any wonder Bergman never made a film about the Irish? Anyway, there isn't even a rumour of any kind of weather in IKEA.

Which brings me to something about which I wasn't going to inform you, but fuck it: the native Ikeans, whom I have discovered only in the last week or so and am trying, with little so-far success, to communicate and build a relationship with. I came upon them during a midnight foray into the storerooms. Right at the back, where there are barrels of petrol and pallets of that rip-hole toilet roll for the staff canteen. There were six of them. All swede-blondes about four foot tall with a stoop that made them seem even smaller. They were huddled together speaking some whiny (like chainsaw whiny) gibberish in between wolfing down balls-meat scraps scavenged from the restaurant waste.

They scattered like drops from a splash as soon as I showed myself. How do I know they are blind? I took a flash photograph before I showed myself. I thought the fright of it would give me some advantage. They didn't notice the flash. When I reviewed the photograph later I saw that they had no eyes or ears or noses, only mouths that ran like zips from the top to the bottom of their heads. They must have sensed me through nerves in their teeth when I lepped out. They were a type of craven, cunning, ravenous creature produced away from sun and mud and wind and salt water bathing, away from all the healthy elements. Stowaways from the Swedish-Ikean mainland, obviously. But why would they chance it over here? Push or pull? Overpopulation/economic pressure or the call of adventure? Now that I have something to chew on, some subject all of my own to research and pronounce on, I really feel things are going to work out for me here, in the long run I mean. I'm not shifting. IKEA is a stable habitat.

As mentioned, you can't tell anything about the outside weather in here, but you can tell the seasons alright, by the signs they put up, which is handy for birthdays and Christmas.

Listen, when are you gonna haul your ass over and join me? Even just to hang out for a while? We don't have to get stoned or anything. I can cover your bus fare and get you a grand feed of balls-meat, I promise.

Whatever happens, please look after Harry my beautiful pigeon, as usual, and don't send him off on any mad errands. And btw have you heard anything about how Lauryn and the crew are getting on in Liffey Valley? Did they even get there? And the rumours of a crackdown in Woodies of Blanchardstown? Are they true? I hope not. I couldn't survive an hour in a borstal. I'd hang myself from high rafters with a Frakta rope rather than let myself be taken in.

A Wall

Centuries ago in what we now know as Cuckoo To wn, during a very cold winter, the townspeople remembered that cuckoos arrived with the first sunny day of the spring. They deduced that if they could capture a cuckoo they would enjoy eternal summer. When the next spring came they discovered the first cuckoo of the sun in an oak tree on the outskirts of the town. That night they set about building a wall around the tree. All night they joked and complimented and slapped each other on the back and boasted about what geniuses and innovators they the people of Cuckoo Town were and how it would be summer all year round and how they would bask in the sunshine when their neighbours in Crow Town and Pheasant Town and Pigeon Town and Chicken Town would be shivering and freezing to death. However, their premature celebrations ended abruptly when the cuckoo, who had no inkling of their plans, flew off in the direction of Robin Hill just as the sun rose on the second day of spring and just as the last stone of the Wall of Eternal Sun was about to be laid by an important personage of Cuckoo Town. Someone or maybe a few people smacked the wall in pure frustration then   with a pick or a sledgehammer or merely a fist

and
                    the wa
ll
                                        that was m
eant to
          trap
                              the cuc
                                                       koo an
d the
          gold

en
          syru   p of
                                                  the
                                                                      sun
                    colla   psed
                                        wit
hout merc
y or
          d   e

s   ign on top

                              of
all of the

m.

A Message to the Dead

Roro's going to send another message to the dead.

She doesn't want the dead to be 'spoken for'. She wants to hear their own reply in their own tongue, incomprehensible to anyone but her among the living. Part of knowing that the dead will eventually reply is her absolute promise never to pass on what they tell her, or even to allow that they have said anything at all. No one else knows of Roro's quest. No one ever will know.

Predictably, Roro sometimes feels the dead come close to addressing her in graveyards. But she has also become aware of them in ancient woodland like Tomnafinnoge and Devil's Glen. She thinks there is some kind of dark alliance between the dead and the old woods in Wicklow that have survived the axe-wielding centuries of man. Perhaps this synthesis occurs because, secretly, these woods are also graveyards, for the missing and the disappeared, the massacred, the forgotten and unmourned. In the past Roro felt so much hostility directed towards her—a living being and so potential murderer—from all about her in the woods that she often ran away back out of them in terror. But as time went by the trees and their allies became less afraid of her, and she of them. Now she is scared but does not run away anymore, but goes deeper and deeper each time into the forest's crackling shadowzone.

Away from the roads and the bungalows, away from the security cameras, the watchful eyes of flesh and electricity, she senses the dead gaining confidence above her. Somehow, through the top of her skull, she sees them fan out from crown to crown, swiftly and darkly, like a black lightning, she thinks, though she knows this is a ridiculous conception of it.

Deansgrange is Roro's favourite graveyard, but only because she lives in Dublin. If Roro lived in Venice her favourite graveyard would be the Isola Di San Michele, which contains Stravinsky and Brodsky and Luigi Nono and Ezra Pound, all of whom spoke to and sometimes for the dead but never, as far as Roro has learned, received any message for the living in return.

The Isola Di San Michele is a flat square of no more than four acres enclosed by Istrian limestone walls of terra cotta tint. These walls are set against the ever-so-gradually but inevitably rising lagoon, with its shifting topaz, then shale, then aquamarine hues, and its vanishing flashes of sea bass and gull. Behind the walls are tall, centurion-straight rows of yews as old and dense and macabre as Europe itself. It is often foggy on the Isola and Roro feels that the dead, if they experience emotions, would be happiest in fog, which hides their shame as well as retaining their mystery.

But Roro does not live in Venice, that city of dreaming miasmas and foghorns at dawn, of languid lapping at the labyrinthine quays, of elaborate masks and perverse, uncontrollable urges, of violins streaming from high windows, of baroque and grandiloquent bridges, of ornate and bone-dry concerts in churches, of twenty-four-carat door-knobs with leonine faces, of marble pillars and marble plazas and marble eagles, of ten thousand deceased billionaire's palaces. That weird city of water and waves where the living are interred in the shade of a towering, unmatchable heritage. No, Roro lives in Dublin, city of the running smiles on rotting billboards. Trick city, edge city, paranoid city, surface city, city of sirens and strokes, city of the second-hand tablets, of the tranquilised foetus, ADHD city, junk-sale city, pest city, bust city, cut city, festering city, wrecked city, locked city, wasted city, bad-batch city, city of the small dog pretending to be big dog, city where the artists are panhandlers and panhandling is the greatest art, where ambition is for your own pathetic sins to go unpunished and sure never mind what happens to the next guy.

Still, Roro is drawn to Deansgrange for the pastiches of Serenissima grandeur she finds in its not-quite elaborate monuments, its medium sized obelisks and Celtic crosses, its countless mildly impressive works of morbid decoration and stony bourgeois self-commemoration. She walks among important people of publicly moderate tastes in Deansgrange, among businessmen, clerics, imperial colonels, wholesalers and high-ranking officials, all who once thronged and ran the minor capital. She likes feeling close to the powerful, now that they have been tamed and stripped to the bare bone by death. She likes treating them as inert objects of study and rumination, reflecting on how all they might add up to now is nevermore and nothing. Unless someone finds out how to hear them.

Deansgrange is as big as wood, or a small city, a ruined city, like Jericho, with all its redolent sites and attractions. It has gilded avenues, busy thoroughfares, quiet corners of reflection. It has crowded and neglected slums as well, which are Roro's favourite, and the only places in the graveyard where she feels there may be something to grieve, rather than merely absorb.

Deansgrange even has its own signposts. It also has mapmakers, no doubt.

But Roro is not a mapmaker, or even a guide, but a wanderer, she tries to know where things are and to go towards them and away from them by instinct, rather than calculation. She spends her time learning to wander by wandering.

Roro's old father said he was looking forward to dying as he wanted to try for the rugby team in Deansgrange Graveyard, which is full of excellent rugby players and athletes of all stripes, he said.

Roro stops at the miniature grave of a child which is piled up with an incongruous glut of toys, so many toys that the tiny, flimsy headstone, the size and thickness of a roof-tile, is concealed. She can't look at a child's grave like this without thinking of Seamus Heaney's poem, Seamus Heaney's mown down little brother and his *foot for every year*, possibly the most mourned child of all time, preserved for aeons in Heaney's small coffin-shaped verses better than the Pharaohs mummied in their gigantic pyramids ever were. Strangely, the toys on the four foot grave seem to be for both boys and girls and to come from entirely different periods. There are character dolls from the latest children's TV shows, rusting models of long outmoded cop-cars and fire-engines, and dilapidated, eyeless teddy-bears that seem decades old. Roro bends down to pull a headless, one-winged porcelain angel away from the headstone so she can read the inscription. The name there is unreadable but the date is clearly 1916. Roro is taken aback and can't understand for a while. Then she decides that the groundsman has simply tidied the stray toys of the graveyard away here, has gathered and stacked all the toys that have been blown about in the mindless weather, because how could the groundsman decipher which stray toy matched up with which forever separated child? It was a good and an eminent decision, she instantly decides, to create this pyre from the plastic scatterings of childhood doom. It has transformed the grave of one anonymous misfortunate into a shrine for every name-lost child.

Roro is overwhelmed by the sheer numerousness of the dead, and by the apparent irredeemability of their condition. Their throats are so choked, their tongues are so cut, their silence is so deep that she feels there can surely be no exit, no way of them surfacing again to the world. Yet she dreams they will speak to her anyway and she keeps coming back to them in the faith that they somehow eventually will.

Roro doesn't believe in God, or ghosts, or physics. Or she believes that ghosts invented God and God invented physics. She forms her religion out of her wandering in Deansgrange. She believes that life is made of seeds and death is made of roots and whatever falls and rises in space and time depends on both death and life to exist. She believes that each body in each grave is a root of an enormous bush of death on the obverse of the world. This bush is as big as ten thousand Amazon jungles and is full of the most incredible hybrid creatures, as well as the populations of the dead. Roro wants to go there, to the bush of death, exploring, but also to return, to be the one who returned.

Another of Roro's articles of faith is that neglect is just another sphere of growth. Strong growth can occur where nobody bothers to look or to tend, among things and places and people that have been left to their own resources. The place in Deansgrange where Roro has chosen to send her message from is a blend of wood and graveyard. It is a Gravewood. From the outside it looks like a landscaped feature, a large, dense copse in the middle of the sprawling cemetery. But as you approach and enter you see how the trees grow over, out of, and around tombstones and graves, most of them more than a century old, all of them evidently of people totally forgotten and uncared for in the present. The decades of erosion and abandonment have blanked or almost blanked the tombstones and melded them into the ecology and the morphology of trees and scrub. It is difficult and perhaps pointless in the Gravewood to try and tell where the grave ends and the bush or tree begins.

Evidently Roro isn't the only visitor or user of this space where life and death, bone and root, grey stone and bright leaf grow into and out of each other in mutual fertility; inside the copse is strewn with crumpled tin foil and empty beer cans and all sorts of sordid debris. But although Roro has come here dozens of times she has never bumped into any of the junkies, who must keep even stranger hours than her, or else are phantoms.

Roro fancies that there are no junkies, but that the syringes and foils and broken green and brown bottles simply grow here, like a new nature, the fruit of the Gravewood.

Roro is not going to even hint at the content of the message which she is sending to the dead. This is so nobody will try and mislead her or anyone else by pretending to speak for the dead.

Also, Roro has written in her notbook that if the content of her message were to become generally known it would be ruined:

The message would become confused, dilated, warped, and long before unrecognazeably transfumed—the dustiny of all circulottering messages over time. Every original reverence shrivels to zoot in the taleing and retailing; at most it's a residue, haunting, onely of countless and ever-increasing. A problem for anyone who wants to speak to future people through their war-time diaries, or to found an everlasting cannibal cult. But it is an airony too because it is the poets among us who most crave and uphowl the questionable nontion of posterity and it is also they whom agitate polyvalence to the nth degree and thus and do their own memory and everyone else's besides. Why can't we have at least some sin tenses that say jest what they are meaned to say to the parson or persnip they are meant to be sawing to? There is romething wsong with the brains of the living in what inflarmation they crave and how they receive, interpret, unemployable it. The dead speak unambiguously or they don't speak at all. The ancients - much harker to the deadtones then we are - had the porist messages, back at the springfall of the messages, hacking orders and numbers into rock. But even that wasn't enough to please Vlad. Among come the courtiers and royals. The stone weathers down to dust, the touchless numbers are milled into soft-nibbed, malleable letters and these adopt and interiorise and hegemonically excrete the gungey multivalessness that everyone now seems so comfortable unaware of. Time's the mad humour of change and there is no artside of it. Sinking in my steam being unfortunately so common as swilling is in yours, as well may you laugh. Because of the reply from the dead to the message would not be a reply to the original message but to some antlered version of it, that is to some other message antogether, and would therefore be unusable. Also, the dead would not know who to reply to and may send their reply to an unconnected place or person, and/ or in a dialect totally incomprehensible to me.

It is easy to say that the dead speak through dreams, but that is lazy thinking, if you ask RoRo. If you ask her the dead could never be that predictable, or ambiguous, or useful to the designs of shamans, diviners, mediums, psychiatrists and other charlatans and peddlers of analysis. Perhaps the dead speak in earthquakes, or falling stars, or in late-night plumbing noises and taps on your windowpane, or through the misspellings you often see on foreign menus and the makeshift signage of beggars and hitchhikers, or slight variations in radio static, or cumulus formations, or the patterns that ants make on kitchen floors and footpaths in the early summer, or the serial numbers of limited edition chocolate bars, or whatever.

Roro believes they speak in scents, in sequences of scents. Because the dead are the smartest, she reckons, the undetectable dead, too smart by far for Homo Surveillance. They won't send a message that can be recorded, copied or retransmitted. But also because the most resonant words in any tongue are the words for the most powerful scents of existence: Fuck, Shit and Kill. Aboriginal urges. That's what I'm designed for, and made of, thinks Roro. Unlike the dead. Who do not get pregnant. Who neither eat nor defecate. Who cannot slaughter each other. They are so very very different, so incommunicably at variance with ourselves. The dead do not speak English or any other worded tongue and their reply to Roro, if and when and how it ever comes, will not be in words. The whole point of words, Roro suspects, may be to prevent us speaking to the dead, and to record over their replies whenever we somehow nonetheless manage to get through to them.

In the Gravewood Roro sniffs the air with intense interest. She sniffs, and inhales the creeping damp, the mossy damp, the fungal damp, the unguence of the life that thrives on corpses. She sniffs out deliquescing wreaths and sodden roses gone-to-seed. Plastic lilies. Melted Wax. And tears, she scents tears, the teary mist that rises from the massive aquifer of griever's tears beneath the Gravewood in Deansgrange, the volumes and volumes of eighteenth-, nineteenth-, twentieth-century tears snuffing the earth's core down there. Roro sniffs the crawling rot of slate, clay, and bark. She sniffs out and inhales sex and sex's aftermath of cannonballs and kamikaze aeroplanes. She sniffs the rust beneath the dark green overgrowth. She sniffs a sleeping old man, an old poet with a plaited ponytail down to his ankles, curled up in a ball in the middle of a distant moon, a small, heavily pocked grey moon that has been loosed from its planetary orbit by some routine, statistically inevitable cataclysm and now just drifts about in endless loss, endless absence, endless disconnection. She sniffs out all the signals that the dead are always sending in the Gravewood and inhales and exhales and inhales and exhales until she begins to vibrate with resonance like a tuning fork, like a warmed-up instrument about to be strummed into melody and a humming rushes up through and out of her, a humming that is not her own, nor anyone's, nor anywhere's and then her bones disintegrate and her blood vaporises and her brain just fades away and her heart turns into a skraking gull and the gull cries down the drumming, tamping rain to see her off and push her down into the aquifer of tears and blood and there are posters everywhere in the city for a time, posters of Roro on poles and in shop windows, and distraught relatives that cry and regret on TV and the radio and the Guards make a show of looking for her but she is gone, she is gone gone gone, gone like yesterday, and gone like today, and gone like tomorrow is gone.

Becoming Polis

Lucheni, the world's greatest artist-assassin, princess slaughterer, shock-inventor and philosopher of police has returned from the dead and been hired by the Becoming Polis to destroy Europe. He has also been granted a small allowance for a general assistant. These are his terms for hiring:

Good English Essential. Romance languages an advantage. You must be a quiet and unobtrusive person with EXCELLENT PERSONAL HYGIENE. We will be traveling companions for months, sharing rooms and other close spaces. Therefore you must not snore, fart, scratch or masturbate while I am awake. I will not have sex with you in general but very occasionally I might, so you must produce a certificate of sexual health. You must be well-groomed in every respect; trimmed nails, no scars or tattoos. Repeat: No Scars Or Tattoos; this is not just for reasons of taste but security reasons also. You must be a person who is difficult to identify or to describe and you must be able to completely change your appearance by means of simple props like wigs and eyeliner. You must be totally obedient to me at all times and in all matters. If I decide that you must in broad daylight take a pick axe to the grave of the unknown soldier or flash your nads at the Pope in St Peter's, you must unquestioningly carry through. Because I am the ultimate boss of the destruction of Europe. What I say goes; get it? This job is not for all comers. Only the most serious persons need consider applying.

Can you play bodhrán, spoons, fiddle and a variety of whistles? Can you howl melodically, and, at the same time, rhythmically stamp? The destruction of Europe will have a barbarian soundtrack. I have decided that. I have been instructed on the end alone; the means and all the trimmings are in my gift.

De Sade, Cervantes, Shakespeare. Complete works of each, on which you will be examined at interview. The destruction of Europe is the being of Europe; giving birth to Europe was the same thing as destroying it. Do you understand that sentence? The Nova will be born in fire and blood and we are the Fireblood midwives setting the fires and letting the blood. Fire. Blood. Fire. Blood. Fire. Blood. But are we looking for a kind of umma instead? I expect you to have considered opinions on such matters.

We will travel discreetly and humbly on buses and everywhere we alight will be doomed. These will be small towns and out of the way places in general, at first. I have been told that the small town as a format must be completely eradicated in Europe.

You will follow me around everywhere as I doom places. You will be making a gigantic catalogue of all the different kinds of doom I produce. For example, if I decide that in a certain heritage village near Amsterdam every pet rabbit and hamster and puppy will suddenly turn into rhinoceroses exploding through the walls of children's bedrooms, or if it please me that a certain stretch of motorway between Munich and Kiel will instantaneously become an Amazonian torrent towards a waterfall, you will comprehensively annotate and illustrate the consequences of such.

In future we will live together in an enormous and echoing hall, a vast palatial Hall Of Reason, and the walls will be decorated with frescos telling the story of my destruction of Europe. It will be part of our hospitality to the visiting destroyers of other continents to ceremoniously and peripatetically narrate my destruction (with your general assistance) of Europe by way of these spectacular animated 3D frescos, which will be the last human artform. In consultation with my own superiors, this is what I have decided.

Are you handy with a sledgehammer? Can you carry one inconspicuously? You'll need one in Italy where we will be climaxing. In Italy the sewer of Europe runs deep and it is pungently leaking at all times. We will turn the odious gunge of past sorrows and crimes into the gushing springs of a new purity. In Italy, when the shops close, everything dies for hours at a time. In that bucolic vacuum, between the shutting and re-opening of premises, I'll send you abroad to terracotta hilltop villages. You'll smash whole rows of shopfronts in. Within hours, dark-skinned immigrants will be mugshot and framed. We'll escalate with other tricks. There'll be lynchings and manhunts. There will be nooses and stakes and schoolyard grenades. You will see just how fluently these things shall unfold. Then, at the moment of highest tension, I'll have you plant a bomb at a society wedding in a basilica. That will set them all at each other with every available weapon. Thereafter the pogroms and riots will spread up the trouser leg of Italy and into the stinking Mitteleuropean groin. Soon we will have a wicker man made out of the entire continent, just as we are tasked.

To be honest I would prefer a holiday bomb in a train station, but I'm not a copycat. And the problem with a bomb in a train station is that all types and classes of people could be killed. It would be as likely to cause a period of intense sacrificial-ceremonial unity, especially in Italy, after which our momentum would be lost, as it would be to cause widening schisms and escalating confrontations.

The destruction of Europe is a noble and inspiring tradition and I pay tribute to all of my excellent forebears. However we must also learn from mistakes and weakness—in fact these are the best way our predecessors can teach us. There will be acts of European cruelty required which most people would not even be able to imagine. OK?

You must not be a risk-averse person. At any moment you could die or, far worse, be captured. I could also at any moment get a whim to destroy you. I am legally entitled to execute you whenever I feel like it, by any method I choose, for any offense I deem an executable one, or for no reason whatsoever, allowing for the fact that *the lack of reasons is the reason why.*

Besides all this, let me tell you something more about who is with us and what we will be up against. You will think it is the police, and/or the armed forces, and/or the clandestine agencies, and of course it is at one level. But if it were only those I'd have let Europe go on destroying itself for another while yet. Factions for, factions against; yes, but we are not merely dealing with an internal security apparatus dispute into which we are making the decisive intervention, though your experience of such matters is obviously on the longlist of 'advantages'.

It is not about the police but about what the police are becoming and about how we can accelerate that becoming. We will be fashioning history on what is hardly an overstatement to call a cosmic scale. As always the world in its chaos and its quickening is my raw material but it is material I work with, and not against. I do not create in the sense of something new and from scratch. My method is surgical intervention to accentuate pre-existing trends. It's all about working with the grain of immanence. Do you think all a visionary like me does is hallucinate? But vision is not hallucination. It's seeing better than anyone else what is actually going on. There is not a thing abstract or unreal about my visionary work. Vision is a seeing into the given and at the same time a seeing beyond the given into its as yet unrealised potentials. We are not just destroying Europe for the heck of it.

Humanity is basically a death-cult—did you know that? Any species which knows it is going to die is unavoidably a death-cult.

From within the present course of Europe is unfolding a singularity which will relegate the human species to non-entity. A Billion-Year-Reich is emerging, visible to anyone who dares to look close enough and who is capable of thinking through the data. The new Omnipower will be based on the evolutionary synthesis of nano-technology, wireless computing, solar power, robotics and the built environment—on everything that goes to making up the modern city. Repeat: everything that makes the city is approaching sophisticated technological synthesis on the deepest cellular level. The city itself will then live as an autonomous superconsciousness with, relative to ourselves, infinite power at its command. I call the power Polis, and the becoming of it Becoming Polis.

Human mediation between energy and technology will soon no longer be a requirement. Cities are approaching Being. Every brick, plasterboard, rivet, slate, rod, nail, screw, railing, plank of wood, underground pipe, cable, wire, every pebble in the pebble-dash is coming to its senses at last. Very soon the windows will literally be watching us themselves, will literally not need anyone to peer through them any more to be able to see.

Have you noticed anything strange in your city? A sense of a massive shadow approaching from in front, cast by a future so excessively dark that its densest darkness is defying time and spilling over backwards towards us? If so, this job may be for you. This job may very well be for you if you are one of the people who sense that, in our European cities, the architectural 'stage' is alive and sentient, but the human 'actors' in the offices and the shopping malls are merely props, and all their business only ephemera and distraction behind which the real plot is evolving.

Who knows what will occur? I have had visions of cities simply detaching themselves from the surface of the planet and going into orbit or spinning away across the universe to settle somewhere else and build a Utopia to suit themselves. And perhaps to replicate and spread around. A whole Venetian planet in my mind sometimes. A Berlin the size of Jupiter! But I have also had nightmares of the cities going to war with one another and the terrible destruction that would bring. Of course, anything I project from my own deluded human make-up onto the post-human infinity is nonsense. But isn't it exciting to lay omens all the same? Terribly so. My advice is prayer. We will have to pray together. We will break into electrical warehouses in periurban sprawl in Bavaria at night and pray to the washing machines and the giant screens and the advanced system Hoovers in there and they will hear us and they will one day acknowledge our prayer.

Back to the police. Nobody really understands the police except me, the world's greatest philosopher of police. That is why this project has been put in my hands. I am a CONSEQUENTIAL RELATIVIST: one understands the significance of a thing by its relations and its consequences. The police are of no interest in themselves (the visionaries among them know this and that is why they have hired me) but only in what they are evolving into, what they are a moment in the prehistory of.

Ask yourself this: what are the Police feeding? What grows larger and stronger and more intelligent due to the operations of the police? Of course it is the machines of repression which grow larger and stronger and above all slicker, less obvious, more self-controlled. The police are the human extension of the machines of repression, which are all, including the police, fusing into one supreme repression machine. They are all Becoming Polis.

Said in a slightly different way: the police are the human avatars of the future city, the Becoming Polis. The City is the supreme immanence of the repression machine. The central functions of the urban—of the Polis, the *Becoming Polis,* are now and have always been to exclude, order, stratify, survey, discipline and, employing each of these functions interconnectedly, to repress, confine and ultimately annihilate the human species. The conscious city is the eidolon of repression. Everything in the future city will have an aspect of a prison. Every space within the city, without exception, will be under live surveillance and subject to instantaneous repressive intervention. Every camera will be a police camera feeding information into the mind made of cable, brick and glass which is everywhere and nowhere at the same time. The Polis will be able to see everything and process everything and judge everything and imprison or otherwise discipline anything within the Polis at will. *The Police and the City will be One* (our project slogan).What I am saying is that the only being that will survive the elision of Human Being is Police Being. I mean that if Human Being is the womb, Police Being—Polisapiens—is the child. Do you follow me? Even if you are smart enough are you tough enough I wonder? There are huge challenges ahead. Could you dedicate yourself entirely? The position could well be yours if you could.

A word to the wise: this is the only possible good you have left.

And if you are not up to it let me advise becoming a hedonistic suicide. Blow yourself up in a disco after ten days on the rock. Better to blow up than to fade away. Get it? Oh yeah.

At Slane McGlowan's Funeral

The waves just kept getting bigger at Slan Mclown's Funeral.

The first wave mealy treacled down the slopping hogstreet toweird us, harly damning our shoes. Dayed ben heavy shovers earlier, sweat code well have been overflot from a dram up a head. Only proles wiv holes in dey soles peed any mind to it, noting how draught-cold and aily the feeling was, like the Divil in Bray on Cursemass mornings.

I've god funeral shoes and I'm hypervegilant. I not things watch are mooned to be unnotable. The most famous hiphippervigilant in all hazetory is not ably the Princess and the Pit!

Its aslo part of my jib as an ol-gourd participint in Sane Mugoink's Funeral tee cess out the wearing signs in the taigiest of irregulars. I fessed right away what this parent trickle down signaled: the onpounding loansh of another dinmented sayaught on Signon McGown's Funeral.

Mose smirked poppers I know beeleaf - in der herd of hurts - that nuttin means nuttin no moare, ift ever dad. I agrey, aldo hipper vigil ants torch me the opposite is oslo true, that everything means everything: any rum thing in the world can stoned for anything else that there is.

So the waves, bay they mateyowers, rioters, pogromites, sperms, berserkers, wild Camarre horses, jellytots, or battalions of matchstick men on flah agarics, keep cummin, and keep growin, keepsteamrollering towards us with evermore hate, ever more sniff, ever more powers, ever more mayness.

In me youth, to the slurpy eyes of Neily Evrycon (though not may), fires had broken out everywhere at once all over the would. It was a time of ruptune and of illambination. Win weeks, multiplesimultaneouscrises stampeded the geriatric, paralyzed, amnesiac order of bastards out of existence. I, alung with the whale of my kind, lost Fear of Police, which was also me fear o debt, which was also me pharaoh might in morphoses, which was also me blandness and eggnorance and animal programming.

So we weir not, we could not be, outdung by the waves, which we knew, at de last, would also be deafated, if not be oss, then by suckseeding goonerations who would, if only baycose it was being penally disalooed, continue the snuggle for Shooin-Me-Goo-in's funeral. Saucing this gave us all the stool that we kneeded: every time a wave broke across us we braced, we took the hit, we absorbed the soaking, we rechopped the lines against the key ops of the scuttering, we closed our ears and our hearts to the clamour and the screeching.

Then, wave in retreat, panic held off, we pucked ourselves up and, basting each other's morale with whoops and shrill whistles and spartang cries of eternal deafiance, we carride on wet Shush McGrovel's funeral.

At farts we were enthusiastically hailed for our steadfastness by the many onlookers who had, as useogle, lined the highstrip to witness, intone an applaud, and (in their own sadmassive way) prataisandpeat in, John M Gone's funeral.

Hoover, as the waves kept caning, copped on increasing their threat, the sidelinekakkaphony of adooradation became a sidelinekakkaphony of pale neck instead. Al flied, levving us alone to face without encouragement the incessaintly oncommin waves.

The steeply slopping high-street is loned with towers of silence, from which no sound ever emarriages. A mill in gaping windows silent with platinumb blindness.

The ninth storie was five waves tall and it sledgevankeshed our already half-hammered pro session, a-felling us like skittlemen and tossing us around like laves in a ghost. We clung to lumps and boxers and to each other's tailcoats, with all our mate. Still, moist of us droned, septic me, and two nobbermen, who had paid Kahuna money to Shun to babel to thick port in his funeral: A DRUNK WET SHINER MAGROAN.

Looking up the nibblemen, I thought about the old mahoan buck in the Shebeen, dwun at the bear counter that was crouched as if hodless, and shootin his moot oot true the back of his trenchcoot. I knew tha he claimed to have once been King of the Revellers. I knew - because he shited it whenever he was drunk and courageoust enough - that he believed that Signer wood never alloy the funeral, and in fucked dat twas hay was sending the waves al alung. Y shir wuddenee? Innti maken a friggin forked tune oot of his neighbour-ending funeral?

Dis tinction does not a quorum make, sow, yet agoon, I was O' blagued to cull a halt to Shovelin Mic Go Wan Ourra dat witcha's funeral. Yet agang I would have to go back defleated to face Shame in the 40th floor ex car park shebeen, far above any pissible waves (though, obliviously, now that we had Bandoned Sham McGoon's funeral, the waves would stop cummin anyhowl).

I world heave to face Slowinmagoin and hem ravin and hexin and sputin like he just lust all fours beautiful doctors in a storm.

I world heave to cane up with a new slop of weareds to try to explain my ongoin foolure to bury him. Yawn, yawn, crystal, yawn.

Acknowledgements

Versions of some of these Frags have previously appeared in *Penduline* (USA) *Danse Macabre* (USA) *Irish Left Review, Southword, Bunker* (Serbia).

Thanks first of all to Kit Fryatt of Wurm Press, for understanding, for supporting, and for taking the risk with me.

Thanks to Anamaría Crowe Serrano and Nuala Ní Chonchúir for invaluable proofing assistance.

Thanks again to Anamaría and Nuala, and to Graham Allen, Gavin Titley, Michael O Sullivan, Bonnie Ditlevsen, John W Sexton, Christodoulos Makris, Eamonn Crudden and Patrick Chapman for reading the manuscript and providing encouragement.

Thanks to my family and friends for, as always, providing the supportive environment in which I can freely create if I choose to.

Thanks to Harry Clifton, and to the Ireland Chair of Poetry Trust, for awarding me the Ireland Chair of Poetry Bursary Award in 2011.

The bursary enabled me to spend time at the Tyrone Guthrie artists' retreat, where much of this book took shape.

***

First Book of Frags follows the multi-award winning poetry collections *The Boy in The Ring* and *Invitation to A Sacrifice*, published by Salmon.

Read more at www.davelordanwriter.com or listen at http://davelordanpoet.bandcamp.com

19648602R00081

Made in the USA
Charleston, SC
05 June 2013